CW00839400

The Astral Legacies
The Orcas' Song

Written by Gordon Volke

This edition published in Great Britain in 2009 by Quest, an imprint of Top That! Publishing plc,
Marine House, Tide Mill Way, Woodbridge, Suffolk, IP12 1AP, UK
www.quest-books.co.uk
0 2 4 6 8 9 7 5 3 1

Editorial Director – Daniel Graham
Creative Director – Simon Couchman
Art Editor – Matt Denny
Website Design – Paul Strandoo

Written by Gordon Volke

ISBN 978-1-84666-850-0

A catalogue record for this book is available from the British Library
Printed and bound in China

The Astral Legacies
The Orcas' Song

Written by Gordon Volke

Published by Quest.
Quest is an imprint of Top That! Publishing plc,
Tide Mill Way, Woodbridge, Suffolk, IP12 1AP, UK
www.quest-books.co.uk
Copyright © 2009 Top That! Publishing plc.
All rights reserved

How the book works ...

Join Marshall in his quest to find the first Astral Legacy by searching for the hidden locations online. At key points in the book the orcas provide Marshall with precise information relating to the destinations that he must visit in order to complete his quest. Each GPS (Global Positioning System) coordinate that is transmitted by the orcas represents a precise location in America.

By entering the GPS coordinates into the search function of a satellite mapping website (read the 'Important Hints & Tips' section on page 7 first), you will be able to travel with Marshall on his quest. For example, these coordinates will take you to the Chrysler Building in New York:

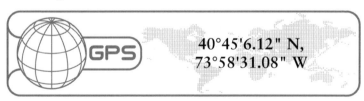

GPS

**40°45'6.12" N,
73°58'31.08" W**

When you 'arrive' at each new destination online, click on the photographs, look at the map labels and open the information panels to discover the famous landmark that Marshall is seeking. This may take a bit of getting used to, but the words that make up each location will fit perfectly into the 'fitword' grid at the back of this book.

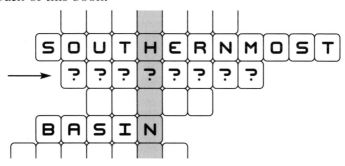

We recommend that you use **www.googlemaps.com** or download Google Earth from **www.googleearth.com** to find the mystery landmarks, although there are other satellite mapping websites that will serve your needs just as well. If you struggle to find a location, the orcas have provided you with additional clues on the 'fitword' page at the back of the book to help you complete the adventure with Marshall.

As the adventure unfolds, keep a note of the locations that you find. When you have identified all ten key locations that Marshall visits on his quest, use the clues to help you enter the words that make up each location into the 'fitword' grid at the back of this book. If you have inserted the correct answers, the location of the first Astral Legacy will be revealed, highlighted in grey.

Log-on to **www.astrallegacies.com** to report the location of the first Astral Legacy. If you successfully enter this final landmark the quest is complete and you will be able to read the thrilling climax to *The Orcas' Song*.

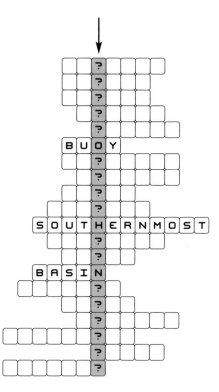

Important Hints & Tips

• Enter the GPS coordinates accurately, including the correct symbols and spacing.

• Instructions for entering the degree symbol ° are on the next page. The way in which this symbol is entered varies according to the type of computer you use.

• Keep a note of the locations that you identify as you progress through the book. You will then have everything at hand to complete the 'fitword' puzzle at the end of the book and finish the quest with Marshall.

• Some satellite mapping websites require you to switch on the photograph and Wikipedia functions that you will need to correctly identify the locations that Marshall is visiting. Consult your chosen satellite mapping site's help function if you experience any difficulties.

• The orcas have provided additional clues to help you find the first Astral Legacy at the back of this book. If you are still unable to work out the locations that Marshall visits, log on to www.astrallegacies.com. The names of the locations are revealed on the photo carousel on *The Orcas' Song* section of the website.

How to enter a degree ° symbol on your computer

Mac

The degree symbol ° is entered by holding down the 'alt' and 'shift' keys and then pressing the number '8'. These keys are highlighted, in grey, on the example keyboard below.

PC

The degree symbol ° is entered by holding down the 'alt' key and then entering the numbers '0176' on the number keypad and releasing the 'alt' key. These keys are highlighted, in grey, on the example keyboard below.

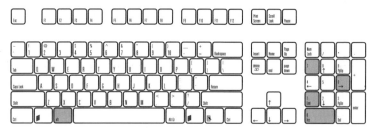

Laptop

The degree symbol ° is entered by pressing the 'Num' (Number lock) key and then entering '0176' on the number keys that appear in the centre or right-hand side of your keyboard. These keys are highlighted, in grey, on the example keyboard below.

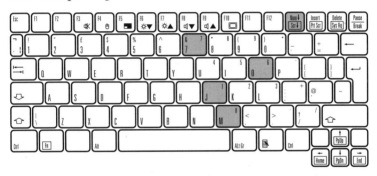

Alternative method of typing a degree (°) symbol on a PC or Laptop

Click Start, then select All Programs, then Accessories, then System Tools, and then click Character Map. Select the degree ° symbol from the grid, then copy it. Now switch back to your chosen satellite mapping website and paste (hold 'ctrl' and then press 'v') the symbol where you want it.

Chapter 1

Missing, Believed Drowned

Marshall Dwight Anthony Covington Jr was unfortunate enough to have his birthday on December 31st.

This was not quite as bad as having a birthday on Christmas Day, but even so it always seemed to get overshadowed by all the preparations for New Year's Eve. Not so this year. His mother, Mary, had planned a big party to celebrate Marshall's fifteenth birthday and his inheritance of $5,000,000 from the estate of his late grandmother. Even Marshall's father had promised to be there – a rare event in the Covington household, as the head of the family, an international finance analyst, was nearly always away on business.

Marshall was looking forward to seeing his dad again. It had been another incomplete Christmas without him.

Not that any of these thoughts were occupying Marshall's mind at this very moment. The big event was still some days away and he was out at sea, five kilometres off the coast of San Diego, listening for the song of the orca. Mary Covington was a scientist working for the Californian Institute of Oceanography and Marshall often accompanied her on these research trips, recording the sounds made by the pods of black-and-white killer whales passing through the bay. So far, despite years of study, Marshall's mother had not succeeded in unlocking the key to the orcas' eerie underwater language. It was far too advanced and complex.

Even though it was midwinter, the warm climate of the south-western United States meant that it was a bright, sunny day – or it had been when they set out in the Institute's power launch, *Snoopy*. Now, though, Marshall felt a chill wind rippling his shirt and there were worrying dark clouds approaching rapidly over the horizon.

'Mom, there's a storm coming!' he called.

'Nonsense, darling,' replied his mother, waddling past in her flippers and wetsuit, lugging her high-tech recording equipment. 'The weather forecast is fine for today.'

'There IS!' argued Marshall, pointing at the sky. 'Look over there, Mom.'

SPLASH! Mrs Covington's reply was to make a slow backwards somersault into the sea. Soon, she was just a trail of bubbles passing under the boat. Suddenly, Marshall felt very alone out on the vast, heaving ocean. Why did his mother have to be so passionate about her work?

Marshall disappeared into the cabin in search of a drink and some cookies, unaware that his every move was being carefully watched through a pair of powerful binoculars belonging to his Uncle Edward, known in the family as Ted. Whereas Marshall's father, David Covington, was a highly paid and well respected public figure whose success had come from endless hard work, his younger brother was a gambler and a cheat who was permanently in debt.

With his creditors rapidly losing patience with his lies and time wasting, Ted had hit on a desperate plan to solve all his financial problems in one go. He would kidnap his nephew and demand a massive ransom!

To this end, Ted and his two criminal associates, Sonny Barker and Thomas 'Pencil' Eddington, were lurking behind an outcrop of rock in their powerful speedboat, its engine idling like a throbbing toothache. In some ways, the two henchmen resembled a comedy double act that you would see on TV – but there was nothing remotely funny about them. Barker, the tubby one, was an ex-con with a very short fuse and a habit of lashing out with his fists. Pencil, as his nickname suggested, was tall and thin … and coldly calculating, like an urban fox.

'What are we waiting for, Boss?' demanded Barker. 'The kid's on his own.'

'Gotta wait for Mommy to get clear, stupid,' snapped Pencil. 'Don't want our propeller chopping her head off, do we?'

'Shut up, you two,' snapped Ted. ' I run this show and we go when I say!'

Meanwhile, on board *Snoopy*, Marshall came back out on deck to find the dark clouds that had previously been half a mile away, were rapidly closing in on him, accompanied by lashing rain and strong winds. The sea began to churn and suddenly, when Marshall was not holding onto the handrail, the first surge struck the little cabin cruiser amidships, almost turning it over. The teenager was thrown overboard like a doll being tossed out of a baby's pram. Without even having time to yell, Marshall plunged into the heaving water and was immediately swept under by the current. It felt like speeding down the giant water slide at the theme park he visited so often when he was younger, but there would be no big splash and laughter at the end of this ride. He was going to drown!

The freak storm stung the crooks into action.

'Can't afford to wait any longer,' shouted Ted, pushing the throttle forwards and sending the craft surging through the foaming waves like a snarling sea monster. It reached *Snoopy* in a couple of minutes.

'The kid's not here,' yelled Pencil, scrambling from one deck to the other with the rain lashing in his face.

'Waddayamean? Look in the cabin!' retorted Ted crossly.

'Pencil's right. He ain't here!' confirmed Barker, following his companion with a great deal more difficulty.

'But he must be!' howled Ted.

'See for yourself then, mister know-it-all,' snarled Pencil, indicating the empty cruiser with a sweep of his hand.

At that moment, Marshall's mother emerged from the sea and heaved herself onto the rolling deck, seaweed clinging to her sound recorder.

'I got some great sounds,' she enthused. 'A baby was learning to hunt on its own and the mother was calling to it all the time … Hey! What's going on? What are you doing here, Ted?'

'A storm is sweeping across the bay,' he replied, smoothly. 'We saw your boat in the distance and came over to see if you were okay.'

'I'm fine, thanks,' said Mary Covington, quickly. 'Where's Marshall?'

'Marshall?' echoed Ted. 'Was he out here with you?'

'Of course he was out here with me!' snapped the woman, a rising note of panic in her voice. 'I never go diving alone. Marshall! MAR-SHALL! Where are you?'

The thugs pretended to search the launch, returning with grim faces and shakes of the head.

'Oh my God!' shrieked Mary. 'He's fallen overboard!'

Everything moved very fast after that. The villains took their leave, pretending to go and look for the missing boy.

'Thanks for your help, Ted,' called Marshall's distraught mother. 'It's lucky you were here.'

'What are families for?' replied the crook,

making Barker choke on the drink he was swigging and even bringing a smile to Pencil's normally scowling face.

Marshall's mother immediately alerted the coastguard and a well-drilled search-and-rescue operation swung into action, involving patrol boats, helicopters and even a passing minesweeper from the San Diego US Naval base. The search went on all day, backwards and forwards across the bay and further out to sea where any number of known currents could have taken Marshall. The search was not called off until darkness had completely fallen and there was no possible hope of finding Marshall alive. He was pronounced 'Missing, believed drowned.'

Yet Marshall was alive! He woke up, lying on a small deserted beach under some steep cliffs several kilometres north of the city. He was spotted by an old lady out walking her dog who, despite her years, scrambled down the steep cliff to reach the half-conscious boy. Shouting and waving to attract attention, she got a passing fisherman to radio for help, and within a very short space of time Marshall found himself in the local hospital with his deliriously happy mother clasping his hand and repeating over and over again: 'I can't believe it. I just can't believe it!'

The next morning, news of Marshall's miraculous escape was on every TV channel and in every newspaper right across the country. Reporters and television crews gathered in a noisy crowd outside the hospital, clamouring for an interview, but Marshall refused to speak to them.

'It's a waste of time, Mom,' he pleaded. 'I don't remember anything that happened.'

This was almost true, but not quite. Marshall did have one clear memory of an enormous dorsal fin scything towards him through the surf … and a vague recollection of some rubbery, black-and-white shapes carrying him along very gently like a baby (though the latter part of the memory felt more like a dream).

The following day, to everyone's amazement, Marshall had fully recovered and was allowed to go home. The press had already disappeared – he was yesterday's news – so the young man was looking forward to a quiet day listening to his iPod ... but it was not to be. As his mother was driving him along the coast road to their big house above the bay, she received a call from the Institute of Oceanography.

'Sorry, Bubs,' (Mary Covington's baby name for Marshall and one that caused him acute embarrassment), she said, jerking the wheel and changing direction like a stunt driver in a car chase, 'there's an orca stuck on Pacific Beach. Gotta go and see if we can get it back in the water!'

The stranded whale was a young adult male – a teenager just like Marshall. It lay on the sand, facing the sea, staring fixedly at him through its half-open eye. Marshall was glad he was there to help the stricken animal.

Then his mother came running up and thrust her underwater recording equipment into his hands.

'Go and dip this into the sea for me, honey,' she urged, excitedly. 'The pod's calling to its lost family member. I wanna record their cries and then listen to what happens when they get him back.'

Marshall took off his shoes and waded out far enough to submerge his mother's equipment in the water. Having nothing else to do, and knowing it would take until high tide before the beached whale could be refloated, he put the headphones on to listen to the orcas' cries. Next moment, his eyes opened wide with amazement as if he had received an electric shock. The shrieks and squeals of the whales' language were making sense to him!

Suddenly, the memory of what had happened to him the day before came flooding back. After he fell overboard, he was dragged down into the depths by the current and only just managed to struggle to the surface, spluttering and gasping for air. Then he had been rescued by a pod of orca! A fully-grown female located him and then a group of young males carried him ashore and deposited him on the beach, withdrawing backwards into the surf as they do when they hunt seals and penguins.

'Are you listening to us, Marshall?' echoed the orcas' collective song.

'Yes, I'm listening,' replied the boy, speaking out loud.

'Our pod and some human beings are helping each other to survive. Now we must do this on a global scale or humankind will be wiped out completely.'

With that, Marshall fainted!

Chapter 2

Doomsday, One Year and Counting

'Happy birthday to you, happy birthday to you,' sang the crowd of smiling faces, 'happy birthday, dear Marshall, happy birthday to you.'

Marshall was feeling far from happy. Despite inheriting a large fortune and being given a state-of-the-art mobile phone, the young man felt troubled and preoccupied. His mother attributed this to the fact that Mr Covington had not made it to the party as promised. He had emailed to say he was delayed in Paris on important business.

'Never mind, Bubs,' soothed Mary, putting her arm around her son's hunched shoulders. 'Dad'll be back soon.'

'It's not that, Mom,' whispered Marshall.

'What is it then, sweetie?' asked his mother.

'Oh, nothing,' said Marshall, quickly.

The orcas had been in touch with Marshall several times. He no longer needed to listen directly to their whale song to hear what they were saying – they had started communicating with him directly through some sort of unearthly telepathy. Their words just came into his mind and, in response, they understood his thoughts by way of reply. What they were telling him was deeply disturbing. It was a story, an incredible story ...

About 50,000 years ago, a race of aliens visited Earth with a view to colonising it. They travelled in a spacecraft powered by the 'Vortex of Light,' a triangular prism containing seven objects from different parts of the solar system, each one a different colour of the rainbow. This prism generated enough light-based energy to allow the aliens to travel anywhere in the universe at the speed of light.

At first, the space visitors were pleased with their choice of colony. Earth was a beautiful, unspoiled place with lots of habitable land, wildlife and plentiful natural resources. The only humans were tribes of hunter-gatherers, living in harmony with nature. Tragically, soon after their arrival in what is now the Arizona Desert in North America, a natural disaster ruined their plans. A meteor struck Earth and obliterated their spacecraft. The precious items from the 'Vortex of Light' were sucked up into the atmosphere by the impact debris and carried around the world, where they eventually fell to earth and were lost. The aliens not killed by the strike spent the rest of their lives searching for their missing astral objects and instructing all the animal species that they met to do the same. When the survivors died, their bodies instantly evaporated and left no trace of their existence.

Now a new generation of aliens had returned to Earth to reclaim their seven items which, having been left here for so long, had been named The Astral Legacies. On arrival, they were horrified to find how much the planet had changed in such a comparatively short space of time. Humans had spread around the world and their impact on the environment was catastrophic – habitats destroyed, animals extinct, widespread pollution and increasing global warming. Having heard stories from their ancestors about how idyllic Earth was before, the aliens wanted to reverse this trend by exterminating the whole of the human race, but the wiser heads among them pointed out that such a punishment would be unfair. It was the older generation of human beings that were responsible for these terrible crimes – the young are innocent. So an agreement was reached.

The aliens will leave Earth alone, provided the Astral Legacies are returned. Seven young people, chosen at random, will be given the task of finding them within a single calendar year. To aid them on their quest, each child will be given help by a different animal species. If they succeed, the human race will be spared in the hope that this new generation can reverse the damage done by their elders. If the young people fail in any respect, humankind will be wiped out at a stroke.

'Where do I fit into all this?' Marshall wondered, although he already knew the answer to the question. He had been chosen to find the first Astral Legacy.

'Enjoying your party, Marshall?' boomed Uncle Ted, slapping his nephew on the shoulder and jerking him out of his reverie.

'Yes, it's great,' murmured Marshall, weakly.

'Listen, son,' whispered Ted, leaning forwards with a wolf-like smile, 'if you'd like something stronger in that cola or maybe a puff on one of my cigars, just meet me outside.'

'No thank you, Uncle,' replied the boy, coldly. 'I intend to avoid the bad habits of the older generation.'

'Then maybe you'd like to see my new car,' suggested Ted, desperate to lure his victim into the garden where his two henchmen were waiting in the bushes, ropes and gag at the ready.

'How can you afford a new car?' exclaimed

Marshall. 'I thought you were broke!'

'Then you thought wrong, buddy boy,' chuckled the crook. 'My credit rating's sky high – especially as I'm expecting a big payout any day now.'

Suddenly, the voice of an orca came into Marshall's head again.

'Sorry, Uncle,' said the teenager, pushing past Ted in an urgent manner. 'Gotta go to my room.'

Quietly locking the door, Marshall threw himself on the bed and waited for his next message. It was not long in coming.

'We began by contacting you through our whale song,' said the strange, unworldly voice in his head. 'Now we are speaking to you directly so we can brief you on the mission and deal with any concerns you may have. Soon, we will only communicate with you in letters and numbers.'

'Why?' wondered Marshall.

'Because this is a test,' returned the orca. 'You must prove yourself strong and adaptable in the coming weeks. The orcas have decided to help you because we do not believe that any species should face extinction. Fortunately for the human race, we have animal friends in other continents who share this view and are also prepared to help.'

'I don't wanna do this,' thought Marshall, suddenly feeling panic-stricken.

'The choice is yours, Marshall,' continued the voice, calmly.

'Either you tackle the quest or, in a year's time, you and your family – plus every other human being on this planet – will be evaporated.'

'No pressure, then,' murmured Marshall.

'Yes, there is pressure,' replied the orca. 'But you must handle it. We will help you. We are your chosen species, overseeing and guiding you in your search …'

Just then, there was a knock on the door.

'Are you all right, Marshall?' called his mother's voice.

'Yes, I'm fine, Mom,' answered Marshall, jumping up and speaking through the door. 'I'll be out in a minute.'

Marshall flopped back down on the bed, expecting to receive more instructions, but the voice had gone.

'Blast!' he exclaimed.

Meanwhile, out in the garden, Ted was slipping some food and drink to his bored and bad-tempered henchmen.

'How much longer do we have to stay out here playin' hide-and-seek?' demanded Barker.

'We're not playing hide-and-seek because nobody's coming to look for us,' commented Pencil.

'Oh, shut up, you long streak of misery!' shouted Barker.

'You shut up, Barker,' spat Ted. 'Do you want everyone to know you're here? Now listen up, you pair of goons. I can't get the wretched kid to come outside, so we'll have to wait until everyone's gone home. Then, I'll knock on the door, pretending I've dropped my wallet, and you can nab him when he comes out to help me look for it.'

'Okay, Boss,' agreed Pencil.

'You happy too, Barker?' asked Ted.

'I will be if you go indoors and get me two more slices of that birthday cake,' he replied.

Inside the house, Marshall finally emerged from his room and was instantly pounced on by his mother.

'You sure you're okay, sweetie?' she asked.

'Yes, Mom!' said Marshall, impatiently.

'You don't look it to me,' she went on, brushing his hair from his forehead. 'You're not sickening for something, are you?'

'No, Mom,' replied Marshall in a weary, sing-song voice.

'Then come and mingle with your guests,' she ordered, turning him round and propelling him towards the waiting crowd of relatives and friends, grinning and waving at him in a way that made the teenager cringe.

The orca chose to speak to him directly for the last time around ten o'clock that evening. The mood of the party had shifted from Marshall's birthday towards the impending New Year, so he tried to slip away, but, once again, he was intercepted by his mother.

'What is wrong with you today, Marshall?' she grumbled. 'You're walking around with a face like a slapped butt. You still sulking about Dad?'

'Nope!' he replied.

'Are you in love or something?' suggested Mrs Covington. 'I know! It's that Julie girl from down the street.'

'No, Mom,' said Marshall, wearily. 'She says I'm a dork and I think she's a moose.'

'What is it, then?' snapped his mother, becoming genuinely irritated. 'You've just inherited a fortune and you're acting as if the end of the world is nigh!'

'You said it,' muttered Marshall.

Luckily, a passing guest took his mother away and Marshall was able to sneak back to the silence of his room. Lying on his bed with his hands tucked behind his head, the voice of the orca spoke clearly to him …

'We will be your guardians as you search for the first Astral Legacy. We know where it is … but you must find it in the way decided by the aliens. We will send you ten sets of coordinates, each one pinpointing a different place or landmark in the United States of America. You must use the coordinates to discover where each place is, write down its name and then visit it in person. When you have visited all ten places, you need to combine their names in such a way that they spell the name of the place where the first Astral Legacy is hidden. Remember, time is of the essence. So is secrecy. You must tell no one – repeat no one – what you are doing.'

'Why can't you just give me the coordinates of the final place and I'll go straight there?' wondered Marshall.

'We have told you before, this is a test,' insisted the orca. 'You and the six other chosen young people have to prove that the future of the human race is worth saving. This is not a game, Marshall. The fate of billions of people depends on your courage and resourcefulness.'

The voice stopped at this point and Marshall felt himself compelled to find a notebook and pen. He watched his hand writing down the GPS coordinates of the first place as it came into his head ...

GPS 1

35°1'38" N, 111°1'21" W

Marshall looked at the coordinates in dismay.

'Don't worry,' said the voice, returning for the last time. 'You will not have far to travel at first. Is there anything you don't understand?'

'Yes,' replied Marshall. 'I don't get how to combine all the names at the end.'

'We will advise you about that at a later date, assuming you complete your journey successfully. All you need for the moment is a grid containing a few letters. You will find it in your mother's notes. It was transmitted to her when our brother stranded himself on Pacific Beach. That was no accident, you realise. One of our number risked his life to give you this vital component of your quest.'

With that, the voice went silent again. There were a hundred further questions Marshall wanted to ask about his mission, but they would have to remain unanswered. He was on his own now.

Before leaving, Marshall agonised over whether he should leave a note for his mother. The resulting letter informed his mother that he would be gone for a while and for her not to worry. The note did not reveal any details about his quest or where he was heading, even though she would be worried sick. He understood the need for absolute secrecy.

Suddenly gripped by a steely determination to get on with his daunting task, Marshall sneaked into his mother's study and took the file containing her latest notes on the orcas. Then, as stealthily as a burglar, he climbed out of his bedroom window just as midnight struck and the party guests broke into a rowdy chorus of 'Auld Lang Syne.' He had decided to travel light – just a small rucksack containing his notebook and pen, the grid, a card to access his money, his precious iPod and his new mobile phone. By the time the kidnappers had executed their ruse and Marshall's absence had been discovered, the teenager was already heading out of California on an overnight Greyhound bus.

With him rested the fate of the world, but you would not have known it to look at him. He lay sideways in his seat, his rucksack as a pillow, sleeping peacefully like a baby.

Chapter 3

Man on the Moon

One of the many advanced features of Marshall's new phone was access to GPS, which meant he could find any place on Earth just by the touch of a button. This was ideal for his quest. He could locate each destination set for him by the orcas once he had been given the correct coordinates.

The first set of letters and numbers led Marshall to a crater in the Arizona desert. He could understand why he had been sent here first. This was the spot where, all those years ago, the aliens had come to grief and lost the components of their unique energy system. So, it was only logical that the long quest to get them all back should begin here. Even so, it was a bleak starting point. It was early afternoon on New Year's Day. The visitor centre was shut and Marshall's only companion as he walked round the rim of the vast crater was an

Arizona ridge-nosed rattlesnake that shook its tail at him menacingly a couple of times and then disappeared down a hole in the ground.

The journey to this silent, empty place had been uneventful. He had arrived mid-morning in the small town of Winslow, the nearest inhabited place to the crater. Climbing down from the bus, stiff and aching from his long night in the cramped seat, he had looked around and found to his dismay that all the main shops and offices were shut. Luckily, a corner store was open and he had been able to buy himself some breakfast and find out how to reach his destination.

'Excuse me, sir,' he said to the storekeeper, a large man of Navajo Native American descent. 'How do I get to the crater from here?'

'This!' replied the man, pointing vaguely to the door.

'Pardon me?' replied Marshall, not understanding.

'This,' repeated the storekeeper (who was clearly

a man of very few words) as he led Marshall to the door and pointed to an old bicycle leaning against the wall outside.

'Gee, thanks, mister!' exclaimed Marshall, moving excitedly towards the bike. A huge hand on his shoulder held him back.

'You pay money first,' growled the shopkeeper.

Marshall handed over a fistful of dollar bills, far more than the bicycle was worth to hire. It was an old machine, squeaky and rusty, not like the swish mountain bike he was used to riding around on at home. But he had no choice. It was too far to walk.

'You back before nightfall,' said the shopkeeper.

'Is that your terms of hire?' asked the boy.

'No!' replied the man. 'My advice. Something bad happen today.'

Marshall had cycled off, dismissing the warning as the superstitious imaginings of a strange old man.

The exercise did Marshall good. With his iPod blasting in his ears, he had time to study his surroundings as he pedalled hard towards the giant crater, looming ever larger in the distance. The vegetation consisted mainly of scrubby mesquite bushes with the occasional large saguaro cactus, one of which had a bent arm making it look like a saluting soldier. Marshall saluted back and shouted 'Permission to save the world, SAH!' as he rattled past. The noise brought a cactus wren, the symbol of Arizona state, out of her nest on the prickly branches and she soon put a stop to the merriment with her harsh, cross-sounding song. Then, a big yellow-and-black butterfly, a two-tailed swallowtail, fluttered past and narrowly missed hitting Marshall in the face. It settled on a tall yucca flower and spread its wings to catch a few rays of the weak winter sunshine.

As Marshall pedalled up the slope of the crater, the song 'Man on the Moon' by REM began playing in his ear.

'If you believe,' sang Michael Stipe, 'they put a man on the moon ...'

'Yeah! Right-on, Michael,' chuckled the teenager, realising that was just what it felt like to be here, in the Arizona desert. This led Marshall to recall a project that he had done in seventh grade. It was all about the Apollo moon missions and he had made lots of exciting drawings of rockets taking off and lunar modules glowing with heat as they re-entered Earth's atmosphere. He also remembered something about the astronauts actually using this crater during their training preparations for the successful moon landings of 1969. And, sure enough, over on a fence to his right he could see a big sign in the shape of the American flag, commemorating this event.

So now here he was, at his first destination early in the afternoon of New Year's Day, a gathering wind buffeting his ears and a small, inconspicuous dark shape smudging the sky on the horizon.

'What happens now, fellas?' he said out loud. 'I made it. I'm here. What do you want me to do now?'

He expected the orcas to respond with another message of some sort, but nothing happened. Everything remained silent – deafeningly silent!

'Okay, I know you guys aren't speaking to me any more,' he continued, still at the top of his voice. 'But gimme a break, will ya? What's going down next? I gotta know!'

Still no reply. Marshall was beginning to imagine this whole adventure must be some sort of weird illusion when his hand suddenly began to twitch. He found himself scrabbling for the notebook in his rucksack and scribbling down a second message dictated straight into his brain ...

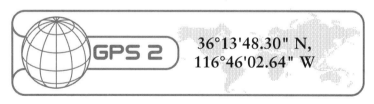

GPS 2   36°13'48.30" N,
         116°46'02.64" W

As the message ceased, Marshall shook his head and his face broke into a broad grin.

'I get it now,' he chuckled. 'Soon as I reach one place, you give me the coordinates for the next.

Then off I go again, like a little clockwork soldier. Good plan! Maybe we'll get this crazy quest over and done with nice and quickly.'

Next moment, the tornado struck!

Marshall had been so engrossed in his own thoughts, he had not seen or heard it coming. It crept up behind him like a fierce avenging angel, a swirling funnel of dust that was heading straight towards him.

'Should have listened to the old Navajo guy,' muttered Marshall, leaping onto his bike with a view to out-running the twister and getting away.

It was an ambitious hope, but just possible. The tornado was coming at him from behind, bringing the telephone poles crashing down as it spun along the long, straight road from Winslow. This meant Marshall had three possible escape routes. He could go straight ahead, over the rim and down into the crater. Alternatively, he could turn left or right and make his way around the edge. At first, he favoured option number one, imagining himself leaping through the air in a graceful arc like a champion BMX rider. One look over the edge at the sheer drop below put paid to that idea. So, Marshall gave a quick glance either way and decided to turn right, the rim of the crater looking flatter and less boulder-strewn in that direction. It was a wrong decision. The twister hit the rim of the crater and diverted off to the right, following him with ever-increasing speed and bearing down on him, however hard he pedalled.

Had anyone been watching, this would have been a bizarre sight – a teenage boy, on an antiquated bicycle, racing around the edge of a giant meteor crater with a death-dealing storm snapping at his heels. To Marshall, it felt completely unreal – like being in a film.

'I deserve an Oscar for this performance,' he gasped.

Just when it seemed that the race would be lost, the lie of the land came to Marshall's rescue. Instead of following him around the rim, the tornado was thrown off by the curve and continued onwards in a straight line, leaving Marshall alone.

'Phew!' he gasped, skidding to a halt with his feet and watching the storm spinning away towards the open desert, picking up objects and throwing them around like a toddler having a tantrum.

After his long night in the bus and now this narrow escape, Marshall felt completely exhausted. He lay down beside his bike, head on rucksack again, and drifted off to sleep almost immediately. He slept for a couple of hours, dreaming about his father and reliving the excitement he used to feel when his dad played ball with him on the rare occasions he was home. Then he dreamed about the orcas chatting to his mother, who looked beside herself with joy at being able to understand what they were saying at last. This happy scene morphed into a worrying scenario in which a tornado was hurtling towards him, threatening to pick him up and throw him through the air like a rag doll. He could even hear the roaring wind and feel the suction on his face ... until he woke up and found the last part of his dream was not an illusion but a terrifying reality! The storm had changed direction again and was heading straight back for him, only a matter of metres away!

This time, there was no escape. The twister struck him like an express train, knocking him over backwards and causing him to turn a series of backward somersaults like a crazed Olympic athlete. He fetched up against a big rock, hitting his head and knocking himself out. He lay there, unconscious, for several hours, coming round to find that night had fallen and the stars were glittering above his throbbing head like a sky full of diamonds. He had several cuts and bruises to his face and arms, but otherwise he was still in one piece. Gingerly, he clambered to his feet ... and promptly collapsed again. He was going nowhere tonight.

Somewhere in the distance, he heard the lonely howl of a coyote. This was followed by the roar of an engine and the flash of two headlights bumping over the rough desert ground.

'HELP!' he tried to call, but his voice was so weak and his throat so dry, it just came out as a squeak. It did not matter. The vehicle appeared to be looking for him, and when it located him in its headlights it skidded to a stop. A big, elderly man got out.

'Done with my bike?' asked the Navajo shopkeeper.

The old Native American had a stern manner but a heart of gold. He sensed a tornado was imminent and had driven out especially to check whether Marshall was all right. Helping the aching boy into his pick-up truck and throwing the bicycle into the back, he drove back to town and gave Marshall lodgings for the night. By morning, Marshall felt infinitely better and wanted to be on his way. But his wise friend would not let him.

'You rest,' he ordered.

Marshall was very tempted to stay, but the

importance and urgency of his mission preyed on his mind. When the old man arrived with a mid-morning snack, he found his young guest had gone.

'Good luck, city boy,' he growled.

Chapter 4

Breaker One-Nine, This is Dirty Dog

Standing beside the interstate highway, hoping to thumb a lift back into California, Marshall wondered if the second part of his quest would be as nerve-wracking as the first. He was an easy-going, laid-back kid who was not used to danger or living rough. He would have to overcome this. Maybe that was why he had been singled out for the task in the first place.

He was beginning to despair of ever getting a ride when a big lorry appeared in the distance and, hooting like a tugboat, drew up beside him, stopping with a deafening hiss of brakes.

'What's your twenty, boy?' asked the driver.

Marshall had heard enough CB radio talk to know this meant his destination.

'Death Valley, mister,' replied Marshall.

'Mighty cold there this time o' year, especially at night,' commented the man.

'Still gotta go,' declared Marshall, firmly.

'Okay, son, climb aboard,' called the driver, reaching across to open the passenger door. 'Me an' Chester could do with some company. It's a long, lonesome road to Los Angeles.

'So, you like country music, boy?' asked the man, whose name was Hank. He looked and sounded just like a cowboy, except that his mount was a shiny and colourful fifty-tonne truck instead of a horse.

'I prefer folk,' replied Marshall.

'NAH! Folk's for pussycats. Country's for men!' exclaimed Hank, reaching forward and slipping a CD into an elaborate-looking player. 'Now you listen up to my country favourites and sing along if you have a mind to.'

Marshall found he knew many of these old songs and he felt happy for the first time in ages, belting out the choruses and looking across at his smiling companion, in his blue and white two-tone shirt with fringes and white Stetson hat. Then, suddenly, the most appalling smell filled the cab, making Marshall feel sick. He stopped singing and, holding his nose, struggled to find the right button to lower the big electric window.

'That's Chester sayin' hello to ya,' explained Hank.

'Sorry?' spluttered Marshall.

'Chester, ma dawg,' said the cowboy, cocking his thumb over his shoulder at a very fat, brown Labrador lying on a blanket behind them. 'He only got three legs since I ran him over outside a truck stop near Vegas, but he's a good ole boy. Goes everywhere with me.'

'And stinks the cab out,' added Marshall.

'That's right, son,' chuckled the driver, proudly. 'I rate 'em on a scale of one to ten. That one was about a six.'

'Hate to think what a ten is like,' murmured Marshall, taking a swig of water and trying to dislodge the ghastly taste of bad eggs that had lodged in his throat.

Just then, Hank's CB radio crackled into life.

'Breaker one-nine, this is Blue Tattoo. You got a copy on me, Dirty Dog? Come on!' asked another driver.

'Yeah, you're smokin', Blue Tattoo,' replied Hank into his handset. 'What's botherin' you, good neighbour?'

'Bears are out in force on the interstate border,' replied the crackly voice from the other rig. 'Lookin' for some kid who's on the run. 'Bout fifteen years old. Can't remember his name. Them Smokies is bad news. Held me up for over an hour.'

'Mighty grateful to ya, fella,' said Hank. 'So that's a ten-ten 'til we do it again. I'm gone.'

Hank put the handset back and looked across at Marshall.

'Why don't you join Chester in the back of the cab?' he suggested. 'We're comin' up to the border real soon.'

Marshall realised the kindly driver was no friend

of the law and was telling him to hide from the police. Hank lied effortlessly to the officer who questioned him and gave a whoop of joy as he drove away from the checkpoint back into the state of California.

'Dunno what you've done, kid,' he called, 'but I don't want ya gettin' catched. Anyone who knows the words to all mah songs is a good friend o' mine!'

The distance was eaten up by the truck's eighteen wheels and it wasn't long before they entered Death Valley National Park. Marshall had time to look out of the window and survey the scenery. It was not a lot different from the Arizona desert with the same rolling, sandy dunes and scrubby vegetation, but the horizon was bounded by craggy mountains and the whole place had a strange sunken feeling, like being at the bottom of the sea but without any water above. Marshall held his breath as Hank swerved to avoid a chuckwalla, a big lizard of the iguana family, that scuttled out of the way just in time and avoided becoming what the truckers call a 'road pizza.' And, in the distance, he could see the shimmering white salt pans with their strange honeycomb patterns, formed by the extreme temperatures for which this place is famous.

The whole of the valley was below sea level and Marshall's actual destination within its huge 7,800 square kilometre radius was a specific sign marking the lowest spot in the United States. He had seen it on his mobile phone and knew that it was situated on a wooden bridge across the crusty salt lakes, some 86 metres below sea level.

Hank drove Marshall to within walking distance of the bridge, dropping him off around four o'clock in the afternoon.

'Sure you don't want me to wait while you do whatever the hell you're doin'?' asked the driver.

'No, thanks,' replied Marshall. 'Don't know how long I'll be.'

'Suit yourself, little buddy,' called Hank, revving his engine.

'Now remember, keep the flies off your glass and the bears off your ...'

'I will,' promised Marshall.

As the rig disappeared in the distance, Marshall realised he was not alone. Thinking this was one of the many little breaks he was given during the day, Chester had slipped out of the cab unnoticed and was following Marshall, wagging his tail expectantly.

'No, boy,' urged Marshall. 'You stay right here. Hank'll come back for you when he finds you're missing!'

The Labrador was having none of it. He continued to limp after Marshall on his three legs, whimpering piteously, from time to time, while still wagging his tail. In the end, Marshall realised he would have to be cruel to be kind. The dog was slowing him up. He had to be left alone to get on with his mission.

'SHOO!' shouted Marshall, waving a big stick above his head. 'Go on. GET OUT OF IT!'

Marshall felt awful as the animal hobbled away, looking round over his shoulder with a hurt and puzzled expression. But it had to be done. He was getting behind schedule and this second stage of his quest must be completed today.

Waiting until it was dark, to avoid being spotted by the handful of sightseers still visiting the site, Marshall made his way carefully along the narrow tracks that crossed the salt pans. He ached to take a short-cut across the fields of crusty white salt, but he knew the surface was only centimetres deep with layers of sticky mud underneath, making it a treacherous quicksand to cross. Eventually, he reached the designated sign and immediately felt the now familiar urge take over his hand, making him jot down the next set of coordinates in his notebook:

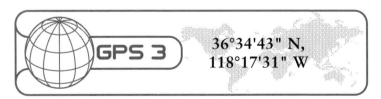

GPS 3   36°34'43" N,
         118°17'31" W

The second stage of his mission completed and with the third one booked in, Marshall felt a surge of elation ... but it was very short-lived. Suddenly, the moon went behind a bank of clouds, plunging him into almost total darkness. Meanwhile, the temperature continued to drop almost by the second. The anxious teenager began to realise he had nowhere to stay or shelter. He was in for a long, cold night!

Just how cold it could get became clear to him around midnight when the thermometer on his phone registered minus six degrees Celsius. Marshall had not bargained for this. Death Valley was known for extremes of heat, not cold. Without a tent or sleeping bag, or even a warm coat, he was in big trouble. His arms and legs began to shake uncontrollably and his teeth chattered so hard they jarred together and hurt. At first he tried to keep warm by walking, but he was tired and hungry and could not continue for long. So, he curled himself up into a ball and tucked himself underneath a small outcrop of rock that afforded him a tiny bit of protection from the icy air. He knew he must not allow himself the luxury of falling asleep. He had seen enough films in which someone tries to go to sleep and is shaken awake by a friend in order to keep them alive. But it felt so tempting to close his eyes and drift away into oblivion ...

Lying out there on his own, about to succumb to hypothermia, Marshall suddenly hated this ridiculous quest he was on and the trouble it had caused him already. He longed to be back home in his cosy bed. After all, it was only a few hundred kilometres away.

'This isn't fair!' he shouted out loud ... and then, several minutes later, Marshall heard a panting noise nearby, getting louder and closer by the second. At first he imagined a hungry mountain lion, down from the surrounding hills, in search of a quick meal. Then he picked up traces of a revolting smell and imagined a skunk about to spray him with a disgusting odour he would not be able to get rid of for weeks. It was not until he heard a familiar bark and saw a rounded brown shape limping towards him that he realised who was there.

'Chester!' he exclaimed, joyfully.

In Australia, the Aborigine call very cold weather 'a three-dog night' meaning they need to cuddle up to three dogs in order to keep themselves warm. In Marshall's case, this was a 'one-dog-with-three-legs night' – but it was just enough. Chester made the difference between survival and freezing to death out there in the dark. Cuddling into the dog and relishing the animal's warmth radiating through his thin shirt, the boy felt himself coming round and knew it would be safe to doze a little, at least until first light.

The sun was already high in the sky when another familiar sound, the loud honking of an air horn, jerked Marshall awake. Chester jumped up and staggered dangerously near to a salt pan, barking excitedly, as Hank's sparkling red-and-white lorry hissed to a halt nearby.

'So there yo'all are,' he drawled, grinning. 'Kin I have my dawg back, please?'

Hank asked nothing about Marshall's activities and gave him a lift to a town called Lone Pine from where he could catch a bus to his next destination, just a few kilometres away. As they parted for the last time, Hank gave his young friend a hug as if he was saying goodbye to his own son. Then he made sure Chester was safely in the cabin and drove off with an extra-loud toot of the horn. As the rig disappeared, Marshall heard him shout delightedly:

'PHWAR! Chester! That's an eleven-out-of-ten – your best one ever!'

Chapter 5

Exit, Pursued By a Bear

Amazingly, the lowest point in the United States and the highest point are only a couple of hundred kilometres apart. This highest point was Marshall's next destination, a mountain peak that loomed ever larger in the distance as he sat on a slow local bus grinding its way along the country roads from Lone Pine.

Sitting in the back seat on his own, jolting about like a puppet, Marshall felt very tired and weak. Two nights with very little sleep, combined with many long journeys and constant danger, had taken it out of him. He needed a pick-me-up ... and he found just what he was looking for in the pages of an old magazine that had been left on the bus. Honey! According to the info in the main feature article, honey is one of the most nutritious and energy-giving foods you can eat. Its benefits were known to the ancients, who used honey for a variety of purposes, including medicine, and now it was classed as a 'superfood' that everyone should eat for the sake of their health.

'I'll get myself a big pot,' thought Marshall. 'Then I'll skip up to the summit like a gazelle.'

Marshall had been hoping against hope that just reaching the mountain would be enough for the orcas. Obviously, it was not, because they did not contact him with another set of coordinates, making it painfully clear that he was expected to get to the top. This would not be easy at this time of year. Overhearing a conversation between a couple of snowboarders, sat ahead of him on the bus, an official permit was needed to attempt the mountain trail and proper climbing materials were required in winter. The gear he could purchase from the shop at the start of the trail. The permit was more of a problem. This would require him to give a name and address. With the state police out looking for him, he could easily be recognised; even if he gave false information.

It was surprisingly busy at Trailhead, the place where the 22-mile trek always began. Queuing in the Portal Store to pay for his food, clothing and equipment, he wished he had a beard like so many of the other young men around him. That would disguise his features. But his young teenage chin only produced the occasional growth of fluff, like the fuzz on a peach, so there was not much chance of that. Marshall even remembered to buy himself a big plastic tub of honey that tasted delicious when he tried it, scooping some out on his finger. It felt very heavy in his rucksack, but if it gave him energy for this long and arduous climb, it would be worth it.

Waiting impatiently, until there was a long queue at the permit office, Marshall slipped past the busy officials and made his way on to the trail. It was about midday, so he knew he could not complete the hike before nightfall. He was planning to stop halfway, at an overnight campsite called Trail

Camp, and complete his climb to the summit the next morning. He had already spent two very uncomfortable nights out in the open and he had no intention of enduring a third.

At first, the trek went well. Keeping his head down and his face hidden from other hikers with a colourful woollen scarf, he made his way past a small lake, an enormous meadow and a large wooded area with an outhouse where you could get water. Eventually, he reached Mirror Lake at a height of 3,230 metres and the view took his breath away. For a few moments, he forgot about the stresses of the last few days and just stood quietly, drinking in the beauty of the scene. The lake lived up to its name, reflecting the mountain peak perfectly in its waters. The bright winter sunshine bounced off the unbroken snow on the upper slopes, which glistened and gleamed against the dark grey granite of the mountain. And everywhere there was silence, a deeply peaceful silence, that made Marshall want to stand there forever.

A piercing shriek of laughter from some approaching hikers brought him back to reality and sent him hurrying onwards, eager to avoid meeting them. He made his way up the steep slopes, half walking and half running, until his lower legs felt as if they were going to drop off and his lungs burst. But he had reached 3,660 metres and Trail Camp, his overnight stop, came into view. He had completed the hardest part of the climb and the sun was only just beginning to go down. He had done well.

It was then that Marshall saw a poster pinned to the door of one of the cabins. It said 'HAVE YOU SEEN THIS BOY?' and showed a terrible photo of him taken last summer by his mother. (He used to tease her that she belonged to the Henry VIII school of photography – a head chopped off in every picture. Oh, how he wished she had messed up on this one as well!)

Obviously, he could not stay here. Someone would spot him immediately. He would have to find somewhere else to spend the night. Seeing the trail getting narrower as it proceeded upwards towards the summit, he decided to retrace his steps a little and find shelter beside a large lake just to the south. This proved surprisingly easy.

There was an abundance of fallen branches that allowed him to build a roomy den which, combined with his new warm clothes and provisions, meant that his third night in the open proved to be warm and comfortable after all.

Drifting off to sleep, he wondered what he would be doing if he had not been forced to embark on this quest. School started again tomorrow, so he would be in English class studying *A Winter's Tale* for the exams at Easter. He remembered how the class had laughed when they read the play's famous stage direction, 'Exit, pursued by a bear'. The others, particularly the girls, thought this was really cute. Marshall had other ideas. William Shakespeare was no fool. He knew a funny line when he wrote one!

Marshall woke early next morning, shivering. Peering out through the brushwood, he received a great shock. This was something he should have anticipated, but it had taken him completely by surprise. It was snowing! So, instead of an easy and enjoyable climb, his ascent to the summit would be a nightmare journey fraught with danger. But it had to be done. Observing that the snow was still comparatively light at the moment, he abandoned his den and set off at a run back up the trail.

Ignoring all the warning signs and 'No Entry' poles, that had been put in place overnight, Marshall slogged his way for fifteen long kilometres through the driving snow, eventually reaching a height of about 4,120 metres. The summit was just under 4,500 metres, so he had only another 300 or so to go. This was the hardest part, but the thought of finally making it spurred him on and, mercifully, the snow began to abate as he climbed ever higher. Eventually, he found himself approaching the flat-topped summit complete with a rest room and toilet put there by the ever-thoughtful trail officials. As Marshall reached the very top, holding out his arms in triumph, he felt a tingling sensation in his fingers as the orcas sent him their next set of coordinates.

'Don't waste any time, do you, guys?' he murmured, jotting down the sequence of letters and numbers that poured into his head …

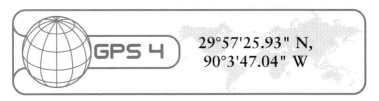

GPS 4

29°57'25.93" N,
90°3'47.04" W

Having achieved his third goal, Marshall felt elated.

'It's downhill all the way now,' he chuckled, starting to make his way down the long, winding trail. He was beginning to calculate how long it might be before he reached the bottom again when another snowstorm swept in from the east. It was not quite a white-out, but it made for treacherous climbing. Marshall did not know what to do. If he stood still, he would freeze to death, even in his smart new climbing clothes. If he pressed on, he was in danger of losing his way and possibly straying over the edge of one of the many sheer drops beside the mountain trail. Then he spotted salvation in the form of a small cave, not far away, in a narrow valley. The sign beside the cave was covered with snow, obscuring its warning, and the anxious teenager was in too much of a hurry to notice it anyway. He blundered inside and threw himself down with a noisy exclamation of relief.

From the start, Marshall sensed he was not alone in this cave. Maybe other foolhardy hikers were sheltering from the blizzard as well.

'Hello!' he yelled. 'Anyone there?'

There was no reply other than a muffled snuffling that Marshall could not understand.

'Maybe it's Bigfoot!' he joked to himself.

It was not until he spotted some droppings that he realised his possible companion might not be human. Moments later, a huge brown bear came lumbering towards him out of the darkness.

It was a fully grown adult male who was exceedingly annoyed at being disturbed during his winter sleep. The animal was startled, frightened and very hungry – a sure-fire recipe for attack. Knowing that people had been killed by bears, Marshall turned on his heels and fled from the cave. To his horror, the animal followed, growling furiously and running on all fours at incredible speed. The boy found it hard to run in his heavy climbing boots and, with the driving snow stinging his eyes, he could hardly see where he was going. The bear soon caught up with him and lashed out with one paw. Marshall braced himself for a searing pain across his back, but it did not come. His rucksack took the force of the blow and was torn from his shoulders.

It was this that saved Marshall from a fatal mauling. The pot of honey in the rucksack split open, spilling out onto the trail. It attracted the bear's attention straight away. Forgetting all about his quarry, the enormous animal picked up some honey on his paw and licked it enthusiastically. Then he pushed his snout into the sticky puddle and slurped it up with obvious snorts of enjoyment. Marshall did not stop to watch this sight, appealing though it was. He snatched up his rucksack and hotfooted it down the slope out of danger.

There were no other mishaps on the long return march to the bottom. He reached Trailhead and the Portal Store again, where he bought himself a fresh change of clothes and some lighter shoes. Then he enjoyed a cooked breakfast before entering the new coordinates into his phone. His next destination was a big city a very long way away. So Marshall called a taxi and made his way to the nearest railway station. He was going to make the journey in style and comfort. More importantly, he was heading away from the great outdoors towards civilisation.

'It's going to be a doddle from now on,' he thought to himself.

Chapter 6

Mardi Gras and All That Jazz!

'The Mississippi delta was shining like a national guitar,' sang Paul Simon on Marshall's iPod, as the smooth intercity train completed its long journey across Louisiana. It was one of Marshall's favourite lines at the best of times, but now it meant even more to him because it summed up exactly what he was seeing out of the train window. The huge muddy river, dotted with barges and the occasional paddle steamer, flowed ever onwards towards the famous old city of New Orleans.

The kidnappers were waiting for him at the mainline station. They were in close contact with the police who, believing Ted to be a concerned family member, had kept him constantly updated about sightings of Marshall. Based on the last known sighting of the boy, Ted and his two criminal companions had deduced in which direction Marshall would be heading.

'I reckon he'll be arriving on the 16.43 from Dallas,' muttered Ted through clenched teeth. 'This time I want him caught and no mistakes.'

'Loosen up, Boss,' said Barker. 'It wasn't our fault the kid went swimmin' with dolphins.'

'Killer whales,' corrected Pencil.

'And we weren't to know he'd skip his stupid party, either,' continued Barker. 'So don't blame us for not nabbing him yet.'

'Okay, okay,' snapped Ted. 'Just keep your eyes peeled, will you? Your lives won't be worth living if he slips through our fingers this time!'

Marshall spotted his uncle as soon as he got off the train. The man was standing at the barrier, scrutinising every face in the passing crowd. Marshall thought Ted was looking for him on behalf of the family and, for a brief moment, he was tempted to rush over and tell his uncle that everything was all right. Fortunately, he quickly dismissed the idea and doubled-backed into the train, bumping into a dumpy cleaning lady who was coming down the corridor with a bin bag full of rubbish.

'Jesus!' she shrieked. 'How many hours you bin on this train, boy? And now you want to git back on! I don't know what's with you young folks nowadays. You all gone crazy, I reckon!'

Then she moved on down the train, clucking like an old mother hen.

Peeping round the door of the train, Marshall saw Uncle Ted meeting up with his two cronies, whom he took to be private detectives hired to help find him. He waited until he saw them leave the station and then sneaked out via another exit onto the busy streets of the city. The exact spot he was heading for was in the French Quarter, the oldest and most colourful part of the city. And it certainly was colourful today. As Marshall made his way through the narrow streets, he found a masked Mardi Gras parade in full swing. This was a nuisance because the crowds of people thronging the streets got in his way, making progress to his final destination almost impossible.

Marshall imagined Mardi Gras (French for 'fat Tuesday') referred to Shrove Tuesday, the day before the beginning of Lent. This was when, years ago, monks and nuns ate up all their stores of fat before forty days of fasting, an event celebrated nowadays by the eating of pancakes. He discovered, however, that the carnival season in New Orleans was much longer than that. Talking to an elderly gentleman outside a café, where he sat to rest his aching feet, Marshall learned that the season of parades and masked balls actually began on January 6th and continued, on and off, right up to Lent in February or March.

'Today is January 6th!' exclaimed Marshall, looking at the date on his wristwatch.

'Right,' agreed the old man. 'So we enjoy a masked ball 'eld by Ze Twelfth Night Revellers, one of the oldest of ze party organisers we call "krewes." Laissez Les Bons Temps Rouler!'

'Oui, monsieur,' agreed Marshall with a grin, knowing this was a Mardi Gras slogan meaning 'Let the good times roll!'

Certainly, the party was in full swing this evening.

Marshall watched, fascinated, as the line of brightly dressed revellers paraded past him down the cobbled street. Some of the men wore three-pointed hats and tight-fitting trousers, making them look like court jesters. Others were dressed to look like the early French settlers who founded the city in 1718, while long flowing robes with dark cloaks gave some the appearance of wealthy businessmen or lords. The women wore full skirts and bodices with big, puffy sleeves, lots of gaudy make-up and their hair piled up on their head in the most elaborate creations. Some looked very attractive; others looked more like pantomime dames. And everyone had a mask. Many of these resembled the famous Greek masks of comedy and tragedy and were held on sticks. Others wore smaller masks, like those of highwaymen, tied around their faces. The whole noisy, colourful procession made its way along at a snail's pace, dancing as one to the raucous jazz band that was bringing up the rear. Marshall hated Dixieland jazz, but he had to admit it went with the mood of these celebrations and suited the people of this city, with their endless appetite for fun, enjoyment and relaxation.

Sadly, relaxing was the one thing Marshall did not have time for. So, he bade farewell to his elderly friend, and pushed his way 'upstream' through the crowd until he was able to duck down a narrow alley and emerge into the big square at the centre of the French Quarter. There was no carnival here, so it was easy to make his way across to the mounted statue of the Civil War general, which gives the square its name. The moment he arrived, he felt the tremors entering his hand once more and he was compelled to write down the next message in his notebook ...

On completing this leg of his journey, Marshall felt a surge of excitement welling up inside him. It had been easy this time. He had just travelled across country in great comfort, reaching his destination without any real effort. A few more sections like this one and it would soon be over. He would be back home, mission accomplished. Then, a firm hand gripped him on the shoulder.

'Hello, Marshall,' said Uncle Ted.

Marshall had never hit anyone in his life. He was a softie, a music-lover, who hated upsets and valued the quiet life. But he could tell from the fierce way his uncle was squeezing his arm, as he led him across the square, that he did not mean to let him go. So, Marshall had to take action – and fast! Suddenly stopping, the boy hit Ted hard in the stomach with his clenched fist. It was a punch that the infamous boxer, Mike Tyson, would have been proud of and it took the man completely by surprise. With his eyes almost popping out of his head, he doubled up and let out a mighty cry of 'OOOFF!' Then Marshall was off, racing like a greyhound back towards the carnival in the streets beyond the square.

'After him, you idiots,' gasped Ted to his accomplices, clutching his stomach and wincing. Barker and Pencil leapt up from the nearby bench, where they were sitting, and charged off in pursuit of their prey.

Whereas earlier in the day the carnival crowds had been an annoyance to Marshall, now they were a blessing. The throng of people afforded him a degree of cover as he sought to escape from his uncle's two henchmen. Pencil, of course, was by far the better runner. He kept pace with Marshall, just a few paces behind, while Barker struggled along in the distance, puffing and panting like an old carthorse. Where could Marshall hide? There were a number of choices – the watching crowds, the shops, a café? In the end he decided against the obvious options and hid in an old graveyard on the edge of the French Quarter. It was full of elaborate gravestones with imposing statues of saints and angels. It was also rather neglected and overgrown, so there were plenty of opportunities for concealment. Marshall crouched behind a huge stone casket, with a fringe of waist-high grass around it, and waited for over an hour until he imagined the coast was clear. Congratulating himself on his clever ploy, he hurried out of the graveyard … and literally ran slap bang into the bulky form of Barker!

Yelling to his companions for assistance, the crook lumbered after Marshall, calling out all sorts of dire threats if the boy did not stop and give himself up. Marshall took no notice.

It was imperative that he remain free to continue his quest. So he headed towards the noise of the carnival, hoping to lose himself in the crowd again.

But the dark little street he turned into was empty – until the figures of Ted and Pencil appeared at the other end. With Barker coming up behind him, gasping and wheezing, he was trapped! There was no going forwards and no going back. What was he to do?

Marshall went sideways! A front door to one of the little houses was open, so he charged inside, yelling apologies to the three young children, who clung to each other in terror in front of the TV. Before their startled mother had time to find out what was going on, Marshall burst out through the back door, leapt over a low wall and found himself in an alleyway leading to the main street where the carnival was still in progress.

This chase, however, could not go on. Marshall felt exhausted and, sooner or later, he knew his three assailants would catch up with him. He needed a better escape plan than just running away. But what could it be? The answer came to him as he turned into the main street and saw the row of costume shops on the other side of the road. They were still open, busy raking in trade from the crowds of party-goers enjoying the parade.

'You've lost him, Barker, haven't you?' yelled Ted.

'Hang on a minute,' protested Barker. 'I wasn't the only one after him, you know. You two were on the case as well.'

'Yeah, but we can run,' snarled Pencil. 'You can't, you great blob of lard.'

'Watch your mouth, Eddington,' roared Barker, pushing his finger threateningly into his companion's face.

'Enough already!' shouted Ted. 'Cool it, both of you. This isn't helping us find the wretched kid. Now we know he came out into this street. So we just have to look for him, okay?'

The other two did not answer. They just stood glowering at each other menacingly.

'I said OKAY?' insisted their boss.

'Okay!' they both spat together.

At that moment, another jazz band came around

the corner, followed by a motley group of revellers. Among them was a young man of fifteen, wearing a hat with jingling bells on the end, a quartered tunic, bright red tights and some pointed shoes that curled up at the end. He looked like the joker from a pack of cards as he danced past, right under the noses of Uncle Ted and his two surly companions, and escaped to continue his quest.

Chapter 7

Do You Love Me? Yes I Do, Sir!

'Please fasten your seatbelts, ladies and gentlemen,' said the stewardess on the short flight from New Orleans. 'We shall shortly begin our descent, during which you may experience a little turbulence. This afternoon's weather over South Florida and the Keys is warm and sunny. We hope you enjoy your vacation and look forward to seeing you again soon.'

As he queued to get off the plane, Marshall expected to feel good. He had completed the next stage of his journey in even more comfort than before and with no sightings of his uncle or the police. But he did not feel good. He felt a bit sick.

'Must be the bumpy flight,' he thought to himself, even though he had always been a good traveller. Also, his stomach kept gurgling, but he did not feel hungry or want anything to eat.

Memories of a badly cooked chicken burger from a roadside van kept coming into his mind. He had wolfed it down late last night, even though the chicken was still pink inside.

'Haven't got time to be ill,' thought Marshall, anxiously.

Twenty minutes later, just before leaving the airport, Marshall had to make a dash for the loo. He was violently sick several times and emerged looking as white as a sheet. His stomach felt as if Uncle Ted had given him half a dozen punches in return for the one he had landed and, before long, Marshall had to hurry back to the toilet where he stayed for a full hour, feeling weaker and more drained by the minute. When he finally left the airport, the teenager had a thumping headache to add to his miseries – but, even so, he was determined to complete this part of his mission before taking a rest.

The wait for a taxi seemed endless, but eventually he reached the head of the queue and climbed into the back of a big, roomy car. The driver was listening to classical music and did not talk at all, which suited Marshall admirably. Before long, they arrived at the corner of South Street and Whitehead Street. There stood an enormous metal buoy, which was painted in bright horizontal stripes of red, white, yellow and black and carried the inscription:

**SOUTHERNMOST POINT,
CONTINENTAL U.S.A**

The moment he saw the buoy, Marshall knew he had completed this stage of his quest and had his pen and notebook at the ready as the next coordinates from the orcas came through to him …

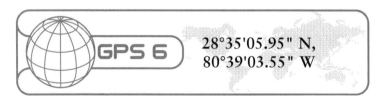

GPS 6

28°35'05.95" N,
80°39'03.55" W

Had Marshall not been feeling so ill, he may well have lingered longer beside this interesting and colourful landmark. If he had done so, he would have been caught by his kidnappers who swooped round the corner a few moments later in a hire car. Pencil had noticed how Marshall appeared to be visiting key landmarks of the United States.

'Why's he doin' this?' asked Ted.

'Who knows?' replied the sharp-witted criminal, shrugging his shoulders.

'Who cares, so long as we catch him,' put in Barker.

'Maybe the kid's waco,' murmured Ted. 'Or maybe he's trying to set some silly record. Anyways, why have we come here again?'

'I told ya ten times already,' sighed Pencil. 'A man at the airport distinctly remembered hearing a boy matching Marshall's description asking directions to the buoy. It's the only lead we've got!'

As it was, Marshall was not spotted by his pursuers and, at that moment, was checking into a small hotel on the opposite side of the road from South Beach. He longed for a hot shower and a comfortable bed where he could sleep off his sickness and get ready to continue his quest. As he was shown to his room by the elderly landlady, he did not notice her granddaughter, who was about his own age, sitting under the stairs reading a book. But she noticed him and was hanging around in reception when he appeared the next morning, carrying his suitcase and feeling much better.

'Aren't you gonna stay for breakfast?' she asked. 'You've paid for it.'

'Sorry, gotta check out,' said Marshall, noticing her long dark hair and big brown eyes that gazed at him warmly.

'At least try some of our Florida orange juice,' insisted the girl, taking his bag from his hand and leading him towards the dining room. It was still very early on a Saturday and none of the other guests were down yet, so they had the place to themselves.

'Here you are,' she said, pouring from a big jug of juice that was so orange it almost glowed. 'How about a croissant with that? I'm having one.'

Chatting to a friendly face – particularly such a pretty one – Marshall felt his resolve weakening with every passing minute. Maybe he should take a break. Despite a number of difficulties, he had reached five of his ten destinations in record time and it might give him renewed strength to complete the second half of his mission if he took a day off. So he agreed to go for a sightseeing tour with his new friend.

'What's your name?' asked the girl, as they left the hotel.

'Marshall ... er, I mean ... P-P-Peter, Peter Allington,' stammered Marshall, realising a fraction too late that it was foolish to use his real name.

'Which one is it?' asked his companion, gently. 'There's no need to be shy, you know.'

'I'm not,' retorted Marshall. 'I use both my first names, you see. Really, it's Peter. Peter Marshall Allington. And you?'

'I'm JJ,' replied the girl. 'Short for Jennifer

Juniper, like the song. My gran's called me that since I was little.'

'I've got that song on my iPod!' exclaimed Marshall. 'It's one of my favourites!'

'That is so cool!' cried JJ, beaming delightedly.

Marshall's heart began to race when she felt for his hand as they turned the corner towards the town. Back home, he had been keen on 'The Moose,' but she was not interested and always knocked him back. Now he was with someone who obviously liked him, so being in her company was easy and fun. He felt himself relaxing more and more as they strolled around in the sunshine, holding hands and taking in the sights. They made their way down Duval Street, a long thoroughfare that ran from one side of the island to the other, looking at the colourful shops and eventually stopping at its most famous restaurant, Sloppy Joe's, for a coffee and pizza. Then JJ took her visitor to the Botanical Forest and Garden, an eleven-acre paradise of tropical trees, bushes and palms. The clear blue sky, the hot afternoon sunshine and the happy chatter of his cute companion made Marshall feel as if he were in a dream. And that was what brought him to his senses. He was not on holiday. He was on a mission, a desperately serious mission, to save the world from a deadly threat!

'We'd better be getting back now, JJ,' he said, suddenly.

'But it's only four o'clock,' JJ protested. 'Is something wrong?'

'No ... I mean, er ... yes, there is,' lied Marshall. 'I'm not feeling so good again now. I need a lie down. How about we call it a day for now and I'll take you out on a date later tonight?'

'Brilliant!' exclaimed JJ, her evident enthusiasm making Marshall feel awful.

He checked out at about six o'clock while JJ and her grandmother were busy serving dinner, leaving money for his bill but no note of explanation. He hurried towards the railway station, planning to

catch a train to Miami, but he did not make it. Ted
and his cronies were waiting by the ticket office.
They surrounded him with stern faces and a
threatening fist stuck under his nose. There was no
escape this time. Clearly, the trio of angry
kidnappers had no intention of letting their quarry
slip away again. Bundling the boy into their car,
they drove down to the quayside, heading for Ted's
motor launch that was moored in the bay.

'You taking me back to San Diego?' asked
Marshall.

'That depends,' replied Ted, coyly.

'On what?' murmured Marshall, puzzled.

'On whether Mommy and Daddy love you
enough to stump up the cash!' chuckled Barker,
prodding their captive painfully in the chest with his
stubby forefinger.

Suddenly, Marshall realised that these men were
not private detectives and that his uncle was a
kidnapper! They were intending to keep him
prisoner until a ransom was paid for him. A tide of

panic swept though his body. What about his mission? He had to carry on!

'You can't do this to me!' Marshall protested. 'I'm on vitally important business. I've got to save the world!'

'You were right, Ted,' growled Pencil. 'The kid is waco!'

The glorious red and yellow sunset was now over and a full moon shone over the sea, making the water sparkle and dance. With one or other of the henchmen holding his arm in a vice-like grip, Marshall found himself sitting in a large inflatable dinghy heading out for his uncle's speedboat. As they bumped and dashed away from the jetty, Ted used a stolen phone to take a photo of the teenager and send it to his parents along with a ransom demand for three million dollars.

'Still think you should split it three ways,' said Barker, greedily.

'Get real, punk,' snapped Ted. 'It's two for me and half each for you guys – that's if I don't double-cross you first.'

'You'd better not,' growled Pencil, menacingly.

The dinghy was fast approaching the speedboat when Marshall noticed a disturbance in the water to one side of them.

There were several small, white bow waves surging straight towards them. His first instinct was to shout a warning, but he thought better of it and kept quiet, waiting to see what would happen. Then the moon came out from behind a cloud and Marshall clearly spotted a collection of black dorsal fins cutting through the water like a line of floating swords. He realised at once what was going on. The orcas knew he was in trouble and were coming to rescue him!

The leading killer whale bit the rubber boat in half, throwing everyone into the sea. Then another surfaced beneath Marshall, picking him up and carrying him on his back like the Roman mosaic called 'Boy on a Dolphin' that Marshall remembered from a slideshow in history class.

Meanwhile, the other members of the pod were giving the crooks a hard time, knocking them aside or thrashing the water around them with their tails. By the time the spluttering threesome managed to scramble on board their speedboat, Marshall had been deposited in the shallows and was wading ashore onto the moonlit sands of South Beach.

A familiar figure was sitting on an upturned rowing boat, gazing out to sea.

'Hello, JJ,' called Marshall.

'Go away, you creep,' snapped the girl. 'How dare you stand me up!' Then she stopped, noticing that he was dripping wet from head to toe.

'Explain!' she ordered.

'I can't,' he replied.

'What is it with you?' she asked. 'Either you're seriously kookie or you're up to something very peculiar.'

Marshall longed to tell her the truth, but he said nothing. He just stood there, looking pathetic, and JJ's heart suddenly melted.

'Come on, creep,' she said, jumping down from the boat.

'My brother's away at the moment. You can borrow some of his clothes.'

*   *   *   *   *   *   *   *   *   *   *

Marshall was just in time to catch the late train to Miami. On the platform, as the guard blew his whistle, he held JJ in his arms and kissed her tenderly on the cheek.

'I'll come back for you in just under one year's time,' he whispered. Then he added as he got into the train, 'If we're all still here!'

Chapter 8

Shuttle Diplomacy

Early the following morning, having spent an uncomfortable night on a bench in Miami station, Marshall bought a newspaper expecting to see news of his kidnap plot all over the front page. But there was nothing. Obviously, his parents were taking the ransom demand seriously and imagined he was still in the hands of the kidnappers. That meant he had a bit more time to press on with his mission. Or so he thought ...

In fact, at this very moment, his parents were widening the search for their missing son from California and the adjacent states to the whole of mainland America. Before handing over the three million dollars ransom money, David Covington had demanded to speak to his son to make sure he was all right. Oblivious to the fact that it was his own brother demanding the money, when the kidnappers refused, Marshall's father smelt a rat and pulled out of the deal, despite the villains' dire threats. The more they blustered, the more he suspected they were not holding his son. So, the Covingtons decided it was safe to go to the police and take their missing person search nationwide. Although he did not realise it, from now on, Marshall would be actively pursued by the authorities as well as by the furious kidnappers.

Fortunately, the foiled kidnap plot had spurred Marshall into even more urgent action and he went to the considerable expense of hiring a private helicopter to fly him to the special island that was his next destination. Joining a tour party at the main gate, he paid his 38 dollars admission money and shuffled in past the huge mock-up of the space shuttle *Explorer*.

Once inside the complex, Marshall expected the orcas to contact him with the coordinates of his next destination. But his hand remained frustratingly still. Obviously, he had to find a specific spot within the area to complete this part of his quest. Unsure as to the exact location, Marshall boarded a tour bus that took visitors around the complex and spent an enjoyable morning and early afternoon looking round the Apollo-Saturn V museum and experiencing the excitement of the Apollo 11 moon landings in the purpose-built theatre. He even bought a souvenir baseball cap, with a space shuttle badge on the front, that he thought would make him look just like a tourist – though deep in his heart, he really liked it!

Eventually, for the climax to the tour, the party climbed the stairs to the observation gantry overlooking Launch Complex 39, a restricted area with unobstructed views over the whole of the enormous base. It certainly was a spectacular sight. On one side, Marshall could see The Rocket Garden, where several historic rockets were preserved, sticking up into the air like big, shiny fountain pens. He could also see the two launch pads where the current generation of high-powered rockets blasted the modern shuttles *Atlantis*, *Endeavour* and *Discovery* into space. Closing his eyes, he imagined those exciting final moments of the countdown: Three ... two ... one ... ignition ... lift-off. We have lift-off!

He visualised the massive surge of billowing smoke and yellow flame that never failed to send his pulse racing. Reopening his eyes, he saw in the distance the Shuttle Landing Facility on Merritt Island, a breathtakingly long runway where the spacecraft glided down to land like enormous white seabirds. Clearly, no landing was expected at the moment because the whole of the strip was covered with alligators warming themselves in the sunshine.

As a final stopping point on the tour, the bus called at the special memorial to all those men and women who had lost their lives during the American space programme. This took the form of a huge granite mirror, known as The Space Mirror Memorial, on which the names of the fallen were engraved in such a way that light shining through from the back made them look as if they were floating in the sky. The moment Marshall reached this moving landmark he felt the old familiar twitch beginning in his hand. Pretending to take notes on the memorial, he scribbled down the coordinates of his next port of call:

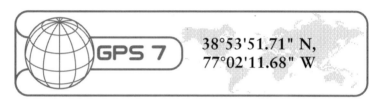

GPS 7

38°53'51.71" N,
77°02'11.68" W

Marshall was preparing to leave with the other visitors when a sharp-eyed security guard, having just seen Marshall's face on TV, spotted him amongst the crowd.

'Hey, you! STOP!' shouted the man, pointing his long arm and outstretched finger at Marshall. The people around him grabbed their children and screamed as Marshall took to his heels and sprinted back down the main road into the complex. Where could he hide? There were guards and officials everywhere and it would only be a matter of time before they were all out looking for him. He was bound to be caught – unless he could stay one step ahead of the game. With that thought in mind, he dived into a building marked 'PRIVATE! NO ADMISSION!' and then sauntered casually through a door marked 'OPERATIVES CHANGING ROOMS.'

Luckily, the working day was not yet over and there was nobody in the mens' room other than one enormously overweight man singing opera in the shower. Searching through the rack of uniforms hanging in a cupboard, Marshall found one that was more or less his size and put it on over his clothes, making him look like a cleaner. Then he grabbed a broom and hurried back outside, pulling his new cap down over his eyes to obscure his face. Whistling nonchalantly, he proceeded to sweep up some piles of litter while police and security guards charged past him in all directions, blowing whistles and shouting instructions to one another. Then, when all the hubbub had died down, he sneaked away from the built-up area towards the wide open space of the shuttle runway in the far distance. The further he went, the fewer people he met, and it was not long before he found himself completely alone, heading for the perimeter fence and a possible lift to his next destination. But he did not yet know where that was. He had to look it up first.

Reaching the runway, hot and tired, Marshall decided to take a break and find where he was heading for next. So, he dropped his broom on the ground beside him and plonked himself down on the ground. Then he looked up, his eyes wide with terror, as something large, on the periphery of his vision, began to move! It was one of the hundreds of alligators who came to the runway every day to bask in the sun!

The ferocious creature did not take kindly to Marshall's presence, opening its mighty jaws ready to strike. Marshall realised that if he did not defend himself, he would be bitten in half. Picking up his broom, Marshall whacked the alligator across the nose, snapping the handle in two. This only served to enrage the creature even further, so more quick thinking was required. Marshall snatched up a piece of the broken handle and jammed it into the animal's mouth. This immobilised the beast's powerful jaws, giving Marshall time to flee towards the fence, dodging the other alligators who reared up at him. Eventually, he reached a weak point in the barbed-wire fence, which he squeezed through with only a few minor scratches and cuts.

He found himself on a deserted road with no sign of any traffic in either direction. So, throwing aside his disguise, he sat down and looked up his latest coordinates, becoming so engrossed in the task that he did not notice a tatty old camper van drawing up beside him.

'You look kinda lost out here, sonny,' said a hippy-looking woman with dirty hair and a cheesecloth dress that looked two sizes too big for her. 'Where you heading?'

'Washington,' replied Marshall.

'Well, waddaya know!' exclaimed the woman with a genuine smile. 'Me an' my sister's drivin' up there with her two kids. Gotta be at a family funeral in a couple of days. Them kids'll be asleep pretty soon, so you're welcome to hitch a ride with us if you want.'

'Yes please, ma'am!' whooped Marshall, leaping up delightedly.

* * * * * * * * * * *

After two long days in the cramped confines of the camper, Marshall's first impression of the capital was how cold it was. He was used to the bright sunshine and mild winters of the far south. Up here in the north it was grey and chilly, sending him scurrying to the nearest outfitters for a warm winter coat. This stood him in good stead. Pulling the collar up, supposedly against the cold, he was able to obscure that part of his face not hidden by the peak of his baseball cap. One or two policemen glanced at him in passing, but none of them recognised him. He looked very different from that sunny holiday snap taken of him last year.

The other thing he noticed about the city were the crowds. San Diego was a busy place, so were many of the locations he had visited recently, but none of them were as crowded as this.

'Is there something going on?' he asked a passer-by as he made his way down Pennsylvania Avenue towards number 1600.

'The president's going on a walk-about this morning,' explained an excited-looking woman brandishing a camera. 'If we're lucky, we may get close enough to take a picture of him.'

When Marshall reached the south face of the building, he felt his hand begin to twitch once more. The arrival of another message at this moment was very awkward because he was squashed up, cheek by jowl, with a crowd of eager sightseers all craning their necks for a glimpse of the approaching president. The boy's solution was to crouch down beside the pedestrian railings and rest his notebook on the ground. In this way, he managed to jot down the following coordinates:

GPS 8

40°44'54.36" N,
73°59'08.50" W

When he stood up, hot and flustered and somewhat light-headed, he found himself face to face with the leader of the free world, reaching over the railing to shake his hand.

'Where are you from, young man?' enquired the president.

'San Diego, sir,' replied Marshall, smiling politely.

'And what brings you all the way up here to Washington?' continued one of the most powerful men on Earth. Suddenly, Marshall felt an overwhelming desire to tell the truth. Of all the people in the world, this was the one to whom he could reveal his secret. The president had massive

resources at his disposal – millions of men in the
army, navy and air force capable of finding the lost
Astral Legacies. Fate had given him this unique
opportunity. Why shouldn't he take it?

'Well, it's funny you should ask that, sir … ' he
began.

Then a passing motorbike backfired, emitting an
ear-splitting BANG! The president's bodyguards
reacted as if it was a gunshot and went into
assassination mode, smothering their charge with a
raincoat and whisking him away. The crowd also
reacted with screams and cries, fleeing in panic and
leaving Marshall on his own beside the railings.
Fearing he would be filmed by the TV crew rushing
to the scene of the incident, he ducked away out of
sight and made his way through the city. Sitting in
a nearby park to get his breath back, he felt hugely
relieved that he had not, after all, disclosed his
vital secret.

Chapter 9

Dancing in the Dark

Travelling up into New York State was a real eye-opener for Marshall. In his laid-back Southern Californian way, he imagined the whole of the Eastern Seaboard to be a concrete jungle, a vast and sprawling metropolis full of skyscrapers and traffic jams – like Gotham City in the Batman comics he collected when he was younger. In fact, it was nothing of the sort. Sitting on another Greyhound bus, quietly elated that he still had not been recognised, he looked out of the window at the panorama of rivers, mountains, lakes, forests and farms that flashed past him in constant succession. He wished he could visit nearby Adirondack Park – the largest state park in the whole of the United States, a staggering 6 million acres of beautiful open country larger than the Yellowstone, Yosemite, Grand Canyon, Glacier and Great Smoky Mountain

National Parks all put together – but he did not have time.

Would he ever have time?

The police picked him up at a routine checkpoint on the outskirts of New York City. The bus was stopped and searched and, despite a desperate attempt to hide his features, a gum-chewing officer in a pair of light-reactive glasses spotted Marshall and grabbed his shoulder before he could flee down the bus.

'Got 'im, Sarge,' yelled the man to his commanding officer.

'Great work, Kronkheit,' shouted back Sergeant Dunne, delightedly. 'Every force in the Union's looking for this darn kid. Could be a reward or promotion in this for us, buddy!'

Sitting in the back of the police car heading into the city, Marshall began to panic when he thought about being questioned. What could he say? If he made up something, they would soon suss he was lying. Yet if he told the truth, would anyone believe him? (And if they did, his secret would be out and he'd have done the very thing the orcas warned him not to do!) It was a terrible dilemma and one to which Marshall could not come up with an answer, even though he had plenty of time to try. He was left on his own in a police cell, like a common criminal, for the rest of that day and all of the ensuing night.

Next morning, at about ten o'clock, Marshall was summoned from his cell by a tough-looking female officer with a gun sticking out of her belt. He imagined he was being taken for the dreaded questioning, but found himself being led to the front of the police station.

'Seems like you're leavin' us,' explained the surly woman, returning Marshall's rucksack. Entering reception, the boy saw Uncle Ted standing at the desk with a big beaming smile on his face, holding out his arms as if to welcome him.

'Thank goodness you're safe!' exclaimed his uncle. 'What have you been playing at, you wicked boy? The family's been worried sick about you. They've asked me to take you home!'

Marshall wanted to tell the police that his uncle was a phoney and the person behind the failed kidnap attempt, but he doubted they would believe him about that either. However, if he went along with the pretence that Ted was really a concerned family member, he would hand himself over to the kidnappers on a plate! Here was another dilemma to which there seemed no solution, until Sergeant Dunne, clearly still hoping to get something out of their lucky find, came out of his office and held up his hand.

'The kid's going nowhere, mister,' he told Uncle Ted.

'We called his parents as soon as we found him and they're on their way to collect him now.'

'No, they're not,' lied Ted, pretending to look frustrated that the police were mistaken. 'They rang me earlier to say they've been delayed. Fog at the airport, I think it was. They want me to collect Marshall for them.'

'That's not what I heard,' retorted Dunne, shaking his head.

Before long, a heated argument developed, with Ted getting increasingly irate as he tried to persuade the police to hand over their charge and the law officers, in their turn, firmly insisting the lad must remain with them until his immediate family arrive.

Sitting on a chair by the door, wondering when all this would end, Marshall suddenly noticed that nobody was watching him. They were all far too busy shouting at each other about who had the right to do what. So, as quiet as a mouse, he slid out of the door and sneaked away into the bustling streets of New York. He felt like laughing out loud as he imagined his captors' faces when they found he had disappeared, but his joy was short-lived because, across the road, a yellow taxi screeched to a halt and out jumped his parents. His heart lurched when he saw them. He longed to race over and kiss his mom and then give his dad a long hug, but he knew he could do neither. And, hurrying away through the honking traffic, he realised he now faced a triple threat to the completion of his mission. The police, the kidnappers and his parents would be hot on his tail!

Determined to get on with his vital task, Marshall took the crowded subway to the intersection of Fifth Avenue and West 34th Street in Manhattan and emerged near the foot of his next destination. This was the 102-storey Art Deco skyscraper that has been one of the most famous sights in New York since it was built in 1931. Squinting upwards, the height of the spire some 450 metres above his head took his breath away and he remembered the scene in the film *King Kong*, where the giant ape clings to the spire with one paw while swatting aeroplanes like flies with the other. These fond memories were suddenly clouded by the realisation that he had not received his next message from the orcas.

'You're hard taskmasters,' he said out loud. 'Okay, I'll go right to the top!'

Given he could use the elevators, ascending to the top of the building was not as hard as climbing the mountain, but the view from the top was equally spectacular. He could see almost the whole of 'the city that never sleeps,' looking down on it from above. A jet airliner screamed overhead, while two helicopters headed in different directions, the THAKKA-THAKKA-THAKKA of their rotor blades reaching Marshall's ears in fits and starts thanks to the gusting wind. And, far below, the boy could make out the streets of 'Hell's Kitchen' – the part of the city packed with bars, restaurants, shops, theatres, night clubs and cinemas, not to mention Carnegie Hall where so many of his musical heroes had sung to sell-out audiences.

Marshall was enjoying this spectacular man-made panorama so much that he felt quite annoyed when the orcas did contact him again. As he went to write down their next coded destination, he found his precious notebook, with its vital list of place names, was in danger of blowing out of his hands and fluttering down to join the litter on the sidewalk far below. Calmly, he took his mobile phone out of his pocket and stored the following sequence in the memory:

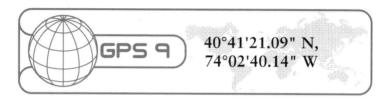

GPS 9   40°41'21.09" N, 74°02'40.14" W

*   *   *   *   *   *   *   *   *   *   *

Bloomingdale's (called 'Bloomies' by most New Yorkers) is a huge, up-market department store on Lexington Avenue in Manhattan. Normally Marshall would have had no intention of visiting such a shop, but today he had no choice.

As he hurried along the crowded streets, having located his penultimate destination, over a cup of coffee and a bagel in a noisy coffee shop, he found himself heading straight for Dunne and Kronkheit, plus several other police officers, who were obviously out looking for him. Judging by the scowls on their faces, they were none too pleased at the way he had slipped out of their grasp and were determined to pick him up again soon. Marshall took evasive action – he ducked into a side entrance of the shop, went up a floor and pretended to look at some items in the cosmetics department.

'Can I help you, sir?' asked a beautifully turned-out woman with so much make-up on her face that it looked as if she was wearing a mask.

'I'm ... er ... looking for something for my girlfriend,' murmured Marshall, saying the first thing that came into his head.

'How about some perfume?' suggested the woman, enthusiastically. 'We have a special offer on Chanel this month. Only eighty dollars for this bottle of eau de toilette.'

'Sorry, too expensive,' blurted Marshall and made his escape.

Thinking it would now be safe to leave the store and continue on his way, he headed towards the main entrance, with its brightly coloured flags fluttering from horizontal flagpoles along the portico. But, to his horror, as he approached the doors he saw his mother and father coming towards him into the shop. What were they doing here? For a second, he felt a ridiculous pang of resentment that they weren't out looking for him in a state of high parental anxiety. He watched as they made their way to the luxury gift department where they handed the clerk flyers bearing Marshall's image. The word 'MISSING' was emblazoned across the top of the flyers in very large letters! Marshall chastised himself for thinking ill of his parents and was powerless to prevent a single tear from rolling down his cheek.

Anxious they might catch sight of him, Marshall kept himself hidden behind some shop dummies dressed in the latest women's underwear ... until his strange behaviour attracted the attention of two security guards who came over to investigate. Marshall decided it was time to leave.

'Hope I'm not going to be playing cat-and-mouse like this all the way across New York,' thought Marshall as he dodged out into the street. As if to prove his misgivings, he immediately found himself looking across the road at the grinning faces of Barker and Pencil!

'Taxi!' yelled Marshall, hailing a passing cab.

'Where to, sonny?' drawled the driver.

Marshall had no idea. He just wanted to get away from his pursuers.

'Central Park!' he exclaimed, remembering that was where some big folk concerts had been held in the past.

'That's just over there, you stoopid kid,' snapped the driver, pointing across 59th Street to the leafless trees and wide open spaces of the park. Then, swearing under his breath, he yanked his steering wheel violently and pulled out into the traffic, causing a medley of squealing brakes, blaring horns and furious yells.

This unfortunate mistake had given the two

kidnappers time to cross the road. So Marshall took to his heels once more, dashing along the street and diving down the concrete steps of a subway, calling apologies all the time to the people he was scaring or knocking aside. Looking over his shoulder, he saw Pencil was not far behind him with Barker, as usual, gasping for breath in the distance. What he didn't bargain for was Uncle Ted standing at the top of the flight of steps on the opposite side of the subway. He was really trapped this time, so he decided to employ the tactic that had served him so well before! Instead of trying to dodge his uncle, he raced right up the steps and headbutted him in the midriff, knocking the startled villain over backwards. With a howl of pain and rage, Ted charged after the fleeing form of his nephew, but soon gave up to wait for his accomplices to join him. They would chase him together and corner him properly next time.

With more than 800 acres of trees, grass and lakes ahead of him, Marshall did not know where would be the best place to hide. Then he saw a notice pointing to the Wollman Skating Rink and decided to head for that, planning to lose himself in the mass of skaters and onlookers that would be thronging the rink. But he did not make it.

The three crooks came after him in one of the park's famous horse-drawn buggies and rapidly closed the distance between them and their quarry. Jumping out and throwing some money at the startled-looking horseman, they closed in on the exhausted Marshall, who realised he would not get away this time.

Suddenly everything changed! Out of some nearby trees came a small group of tough-looking skinheads on BMX bikes. They skidded to a halt beside the three kidnappers, brandishing chains and coshes and demanding money. Marshall could not believe his eyes. The villains were being mugged! They were victims of crime themselves!

'What goes around, comes around,' chuckled Marshall, jogging away down a long path leading out of the park. Outside the gates, he jumped onto a waiting bus, not caring where it took him so long as it was away from his pursuers.

*   *   *   *   *   *   *   *   *   *   *

After a long stop-start ride, the bus deposited Marshall outside the main entrance of the Bronx Zoo. Feeling tired and hungry, he decided to kill the next two or three hours there before continuing his journey once it got dark. He bought himself a ticket, freshened up in the mens' room, pigged out on a double cheeseburger with large fries and then set off to see the animals, guidebook in hand.

His first port of call was the rainforest enclosure that was home to a wide variety of creatures, including some chattering gibbons who swung through the dense green foliage with effortless ease. Then he moved on to Tiger Mountain, where he gazed in awe at a white Siberian tiger and chuckled at the antics of a rescued snow leopard cub who was playing with a piece of rope. Following a disappointing tour of the aquarium (there were no orcas), Marshall ended up in the Congo Forest, looking at a massive lowland gorilla who was casually chewing on a tasty shoot held in its hand like a stick of toffee.

'Handsome sorta fella, ain't he?' commented the man standing next to him beside the railing.

'Reminds me of my geography teacher, Mr Matthews,' joked Marshall.

The man laughed and looked more closely at the boy beside him.

'Hey! Don't I know you?' he exclaimed.

'I don't think so,' replied Marshall with a polite shake of his head.

'Yes, I know your face,' insisted the man. 'Now where have I seen it before ...?'

Marshall realised he was in trouble just at the same moment the man remembered who he was.

'You're that kid who's on the run!' cried the

man. 'I saw your picture down at the station!'

Marshall had taken to his heels and was fleeing towards the exit before the man had even finished speaking.

'Of all the luck,' he cursed, charging outside into the rapidly gathering darkness. 'Why did I have to stand next to an off-duty policeman of all people!'

Knowing the man would soon alert the authorities to his current whereabouts, Marshall wanted to get away from this area as soon as possible. He was still deciding what would be the quickest and safest way to do this when all the lights went out!

'What's going on?' he asked out loud.

'Looks like a powercut, kiddo,' answered a passing traffic warden. 'We gits them here from time to time.'

This, however, was no local blackout. It was a city-wide power failure that plunged the whole of New York into complete darkness, causing total chaos. Traffic ground to a halt, blocking all the roads. The subway stopped. So did the ferries.

Computers crashed and televisions fell silent. Offices, shops and factories were forced to close, causing millions of people to pour onto the streets, all looking bewildered and wondering how they were going to get home. It was like the end of the world – a foretaste of what might happen if Marshall failed in his quest.

Hurrying down a crowded Bronx shopping mall, the teenager wondered what on earth could go wrong next. The orcas had warned him that the task ahead would be taxing – but he had not realised it would test him right to the limit!

'What do I do now?' he asked himself. 'I've got to get all the way to Liberty Island with no means of transport in complete and utter darkness!'

Then he had a brainwave! He saw a candlelit shop selling rollerboots and other street-skating equipment.

'Hang on, mister,' he yelled to the shopkeeper, who was about to close the door. 'I wanna buy some gear! I can pay cash.'

Twenty minutes later, Marshall emerged wearing
a pair of the latest in-line skates, a streamlined
speed helmet, some knee pads and some elbow
guards. He also carried a detailed map of the city
and a thin torch with an extra-powerful beam.
Now he had everything he needed to complete his
stay in 'The Big Apple' and hopefully reach the end
of his quest.

Feeling light-headed with excitement, Marshall
swooped and swerved his way through the crowds,
following the main road back into Manhattan.
The speed at which he was travelling and the
graceful, swaying curves he made from side to side
to keep up his momentum made it feel as if he was
dancing in the dark. Hardly slowing down at the
gridlocked junctions, his whirring skates swiftly
carried him right to the skyscraper zone in the heart
of the city.

'This is so cool!' he chuckled to himself, realising
he was the one person in the whole of New York

for whom this powercut was a blessing. His pursuers had absolutely no hope whatsoever of finding him in the pitch blackness.

At half past three in the morning, the lights suddenly all came on again. Marshall did not mind. He had reached his destination, the ferry terminal in Battery Park through which all visitors to the island must pass. Exhausted by his exertions, he lay down on a bench and dozed fitfully until dawn. When he woke, he made sure he was first in the queue for the ferry – until he read a notice warning that airport-type security would be in operation to deter possible terrorist attacks. Marshall's heart sank.

He had come so far. Surely he couldn't fail now. He decided not to hang around and find out. Hurrying down to the waterfront, he enquired of the boatmen if any of them would be prepared to take him to the island. One man agreed for an exorbitant price, but Marshall did not care. It was now or never!

Sailing around the foot of the gigantic statue, Marshall preyed that the orcas would send him their next message – but, of course, it did not come.

'Hey, mister,' he yelled to the boatman. 'Put me ashore will you, please?'

'It ain't allowed!' replied the man.

'Who's picking up the tab here!' retorted Marshall, sharply.

He was already considerably out of pocket, so it was very much a case of 'who pays the piper calls the tune!'

'I can set you down over there,' muttered the boatman, pointing to some stone steps around which the water was lapping. 'Five minutes only, mind.'

'That's all I need, thanks,' called Marshall.

Standing on the island with America's world-famous statement of freedom towering above his head, Marshall's thoughts flitted to the millions of desperate immigrants who had sailed past this statue, seeing in it a symbol of hope. Then his mind turned to the other less fortunate mortals who had been brought to America in filthy, overcrowded slave ships, destined for a life of misery and toil. No wonder the aliens wished to wipe out humanity. Not only had humankind abused the flora and fauna of planet Earth, it had also practised the most appalling cruelty on its fellow beings.

Marshall's unhappy thoughts ended here. Next moment, his hand began to twitch again and he locked the following coordinates into his mobile phone for quickness …

GPS 10   43°04'38.10" N, 79°04'31.30" W

They came just in time. Spotting a police patrol vessel in the far distance, the boatman shouted to Marshall that they must leave immediately, so they set off to the New Jersey side of the river that was much closer to hand. Marshall did not mind. His business in the city was done. He scrambled up the quayside steps and set off for the subway station.

'So long, New York,' he sang. 'It's bin good to know ya!'

Chapter 10

The Fall Guy

Marshall knew he was being caught on CCTV as he entered the main hall of the big bus station and bought a ticket to his final destination by the Canadian border. He even stopped for a moment to give the cameras a better look, bending down and pretending to tie up his shoelace, before looking all around and slowly leaving the building.

'I give it five minutes before those pictures are being beamed to police HQ in New York,' he thought. 'Then all hell will be let loose – but they won't find me where they think they're gonna find me!'

Hurrying away from the bus station towards the State highway that ran north, Marshall's plan was to let the authorities think he was on the bus, whereas he was really planning to hitch a lift to a famous natural wonder near Buffalo city. And it was not long before he managed to thumb a ride in a smart-looking dark saloon driven by a middle-aged man with a stiff, almost military manner. Marshall was well aware of the dangers of getting into cars with people he did not know, but he was determined to complete his quest and this man had an air of the utmost respectability about him. He looked like some kind of government official or administrator.

'Where are you trying to get to, young man?' asked the driver.

'Anywhere north, sir,' answered Marshall in his politest voice.

'I'm heading for the Falls,' continued the man. 'Is that any good to you?'

'Perfect, thank you,' said Marshall, barely able to conceal his excitement at being taken exactly where he wanted to go.

The pair drove in silence for ten minutes or more.

Eventually, the driver looked across and acknowledged the presence of his young passenger.

'My name's Wilson,' he said, 'Police Commissioner Rodney Wilson. And you are?'

'Daniel Watts,' lied Marshall, smoothly. 'My friends all call me Danny.'

'Then I'll do the same, Danny,' said the policeman with a friendly smile. 'I'm Rod to my friends.'

So the conversation began with the high-ranking police official being completely open and honest to his young companion and Marshall lying through his teeth with every word he uttered.

Eventually, the reason for the man's journey came up.

'This is my first day in the job,' he explained. 'I've just been transferred up here from Philadelphia. They haven't given me the full brief yet, but it seems I have to oversee the recapture of some elusive teenager who's been running rings round the New York State Police Department. Made complete fools of them, so I'm told, and he's still free. But not for much longer. We've been tipped off that he's on a Greyhound heading this way, so we're setting up a nice big reception committee for him. The press are going to be there, too.'

Marshall kept up the pretence for the whole of the journey. Eventually, as they drew into the car park on the American side of the Falls, Marshall saw the Greyhound surrounded by numerous police cars and swarming with police officers. A police sergeant hurried over to the dark saloon and saluted in a respectful fashion.

'Cut the formalities, Sergeant,' said the commissioner, curtly. 'Just cut to the chase. Have you caught this kid yet?'

'No, sir,' replied the sergeant, looking highly embarrassed. 'Our intelligence was wrong. He wasn't on the bus.'

'I don't believe this!' snapped Wilson, getting out of the car. 'The press are going to have a field-day. What does this wretched child look like anyway?'

''Bout fifteen years old, sir,' answered the sergeant. 'Slim build. Blonde hair. Here's a picture of him ...'

The penny dropped before the sergeant had even shown him the photograph. His mouth dropping open in disbelief, Commissioner Wilson turned round to find the passenger door of his car wide open and no sign of his young travelling companion.

'Of all the bare-faced cheek!' he shouted, stamping his foot so hard on the ground that he hurt his knee.

Joining some of the thousands of visitors who throng to this site every day, Marshall could not help but giggle when he thought of how he had duped one of New York State's top policemen. But his glee only lasted for a few moments. Standing by the entrance to American Falls were his mother and father. Also, in a nearby car, sat the three kidnappers with Uncle Ted bobbing his head up and down like a jack-in-the-box to avoid being seen by his brother. If Marshall went any further, one or the other would be bound to spot him. And he imagined he would need to get closer to the water before the orcas noted his tenth successful visit and advised him how to complete the search for the first Astral Legacy. Thinking on his feet, Marshall jumped on board a minibus that took visitors round to Horseshoe Falls, the equally impressive waterfall on the Canadian side of the border.

That's when it all went wrong! Hurrying towards the entrance to The Journey Beneath The Falls (a series of scenic tunnels leading right under the thundering water), Marshall slipped on a half-eaten ice cream and fell over, twisting his ankle. A small crowd gathered round and helped him to his feet, attracting the attention of a Canadian police officer, who hurried over to see if he could be of any assistance.

'You okay, kid?' he asked.

'Sure,' replied Marshall, through clenched teeth.

'You don't look so clever to me,' continued the officer. 'Lemme see that ankle.'

'It's fine, thanks!' insisted Marshall, almost shouting.

'Hey, wait a minute!' exclaimed the policeman, looking at the boy's face for the first time. 'Ain't you the kid that all this fuss is about ...'

Marshall's answer was to push his way through the crowd and make off – but only at a hobble! He was a wounded animal and the net was closing around him fast.

News of the sighting soon reached the American side of the Falls. It was followed by a mass exodus of police, parents, kidnappers and press from one side of the border to the other, all acting independently and unaware they were chasing the same quarry. Meanwhile, looking anxiously over his shoulder, Marshall waited impatiently in the long queue to buy a ticket for going under the waterfall. Seeing his pursuers arriving one by one and looking around for him intently, he lost his nerve and jumped the entrance barrier. This was a foolish thing to do on two counts. Firstly, the yells of protest and screams of alarm from the people in the queue pinpointed where he was. Secondly, he landed heavily on his injured ankle, doubling the pain and making it almost impossible for him to stand on it, let alone run. But run he did, gritting his teeth and charging as fast as he could down the brightly lit tourist tunnels under the Falls. He could hear the roar of the water as he got nearer the centre and then, at the worst possible moment, an orca chose to speak to him again as it had done in his bedroom all those weeks before.

'You have done well, Marshall,' said the voice in his head. 'To find the first Astral Legacy, take the names of the ten places you have visited and fit them into the grid that was hidden in your mother's notes. The letters already in place indicate which word to use on each line. When you have finished, the middle section, reading downwards, will spell the name of the place where your object is hidden. The only further clue we will give you is that your ultimate destination has something to do with light.'

Marshall was in so much pain and so anxious about all the people charging after him that he barely took in what the orca had said.

'Can you run that past me again?' he shouted above the deafening roar of the water. 'I'm not quite sure …'

But there was silence in his head. This game was being played at the highest level. You had to get everything right first time. There were no second chances!

The kidnappers were the first to catch up with him at an open gallery looking out at the foaming torrent of water.

'There he is!' yelled Ted. 'Grab him!'

'We'll get caught in the act!' protested Pencil.

'Not if we're quick!' retorted Ted, even more desperate to get his hands on some money after the long and expensive chase.

He was too late!

'Good grief!' exclaimed Mr Covington, hurrying around the corner with his wife. 'What the hell are you doing here, Ted?'

'Same as you, bro,' replied Ted, quickly. 'Bin

doin' my level best to locate my missing nephew.'

This brief conversation gave Marshall time to dash in the opposite direction, looking for an escape route. But there was none!

Around the other corner charged a hot and irate-looking Commissioner Wilson, followed by a whole posse of policemen and reporters. The fugitive was finally trapped! His pursuers were closing in on him from either side and there was no way out now.

Or was there? Marshall remembered reading once that many daredevils had thrown themselves over the Falls, often in a barrel, and lived to tell the tale. So, before anyone realised what he was doing, he leaped over the safety barriers and hobbled to the edge of the precipice.

'If I fail to find my Astral Legacy,' he thought, 'at least I will have died trying.'

With that, he launched himself into the unknown.

What happens next?

When you have identified the ten key locations that Marshall visits on his quest, use the orcas' clues to help you place them into the fitword grid on the next page. If you insert the words of the answers correctly, the location of the first Astral Legacy will be revealed, highlighted in grey.

Then log on to www.astrallegacies.com to report the location of the first legacy. If you successfully enter this final landmark into the website, the adventure is complete and you will be able to read the thrilling climax to *The Orca's Song* online.

**Read the book ... find the hidden locations ...
solve the puzzle ... save the world!**
www.astrallegacies.com

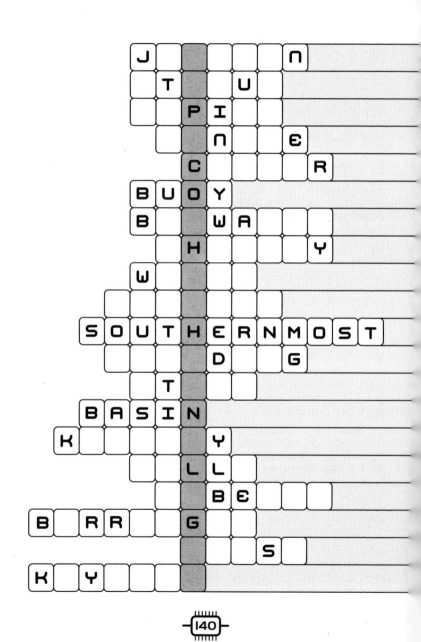

GPS CODE 4 – A famous square in the centre of New Orleans.

GPS CODE 9 – A cast figure of a person.

GPS CODE 8 – The tallest building in New York.

GPS CODE 6 – A point in the middle of something.

GPS CODE 1 – A large hollow caused by an impact.

GPS CODE 5 – A floating object that marks a navigation point for boats.

GPS CODE 2 – Naughty H_2O

GPS CODE 3 – The name of a mountain that Marshall visits on his quest.

GPS CODE 7 – The colour of milk.

GPS CODE 10 – The most famous 'falls' in America.

GPS CODE 5 – The opposite of northernmost.

GPS CODE 8 – A structure with walls and a roof.

GPS CODE 8 – There are 50 of these in America.

GPS CODE 2 – A circular valley or natural depression in the landscape.

GPS CODE 6 – Thirty-fifth President of the United States.

GPS CODE 10 – Collapses to the ground.

GPS CODE 9 – A very famous statue on Ellis Island, New York.

GPS CODE 1 – The location of a meteor impact, in the Arizona desert.

GPS CODE 7 – A building for people to live in.

GPS CODE 5 – This place includes the southernmost point in the USA.

Available from all good bookshops!

The Tigers' Secret

After accepting the tigers' challenge to find the second Astral Legacy, Asha is whisked into an adventure beyond her wildest imaginings. You can follow the GPS coordinates and travel with Asha into the depths of Asia.

Solving the final puzzle will yield the location of the second Astral Legacy and will enable you to unlock the conclusion to the adventure on www.astrallegacies.com

About the Author

Gordon Volke's commercial writing career began in 1972 when he was responsible for inventing the comic antics of Dennis the Menace, Minnie the Minx and The Bash Street Kids in the UK's best-selling comic, *The Beano*.

Since this auspicious start to his writing career, Gordon has gained plaudits by originating material for Snoopy (Peanuts), Tom and Jerry, Popeye and Garfield, and has been the principal contributor for numerous comics and magazines, including *Twinkle*, *Thomas the Tank Engine*, *The James Bond Experience* and *Jurassic Park*.

In 1998, Gordon began writing for *The Tweenies*, the Bafta award-winning pre-school series, scripting 44 of the 365 episodes.

Over the years Gordon has originated children's books covering most genres and age categories. He lives near Brighton on the south coast of England.